KT-513-746

Barnet
Herts.
EN5 4QT
Tel: 020 8359 4040

1 3 FEB 2017

Please return/renew this item by the
last date shown to avoid a charge.
Books may also be renewed by phone
and Internet. May not be renewed if
required by another reader.

www.libraries.barnet.gov.uk

BARNET
LONDON BOROUGH

30131 05512730 9

LONDON BOROUGH OF BARNET

ALSO BY KIRSTY LOGAN

The Rental Heart and Other Fairytales
The Gracekeepers

KIRSTY LOGAN

A Portable Shelter

VINTAGE

1 3 5 7 9 10 8 6 4 2

Vintage
20 Vauxhall Bridge Road,
London SW1V 2SA

Vintage is part of the Penguin Random House
group of companies whose addresses can be found at
global.penguinrandomhouse.com

Copyright © Kristy Logan 2015

Kirsty Logan has asserted her right to be identified as the
author of this Work in accordance with the Copyright,
Designs and Patents Act 1988

First published in Vintage in 2016

First published in hardback by The Association for
Scottish Literary Studies in 2015

penguin.co.uk/vintage

A CIP catalogue record for this book is available
from the British Library

ISBN 9781784702342

Typeset in India by Thomson Digital Pvt Ltd, Noida, Delhi

Printed and bound in Great Britain by Clays Ltd, St Ives plc

Penguin Random House is committed to a sustainable future
for our business, our readers and our planet. This book is made
from Forest Stewardship Council® certified paper.

MIX
Paper from
responsible sources
FSC
www.fsc.org   FSC® C018179

To Dad –

for taking me to the great, grey, green, greasy Limpopo river
all set about with fever trees

It doesn't matter who my father was. It matters who
I remember he was.

— ANNE SEXTON

There is a crack in everything. That's how the light gets in.

— LEONARD COHEN

Contents

Ruth:

I'm going to tell you a story. You just stay there, warm and cosy, all cooried in. I brought you here to this little house at the top of the world because – well, because you are inside me, so everywhere I go you must go too. But I came here with your other mother so we could make ourselves a shelter. Somewhere safe and steady as the beat of a heart. Can you hear our home? The wind, the waves, the seabirds crying? The shutters rattle like bones and the sea growls as it swallows the land. But don't you worry. We'll stay quiet in this patch of light, and everything will be fine.

It's just the two of us here now. Your other mother is busy at work, many miles away, turning reality into stories so it can be shared. At this moment her voice is being heard by thousands of people, while mine is heard only by you. And honestly, I don't even know if you have ears yet. So perhaps I am talking only to myself.

I can't see you, but sometimes I can feel you. You're a part of me, but still you're a stranger to me. Soon we will meet, and you will see that the world can be cold and difficult. We can't always have what we want. And what we want and what is good for us aren't the same thing.

1

But I will make sure that you know something more important: at the end, no matter what happens, you'll always be loved. Before I loved you, I loved your other mother. She'll be my last love, but she wasn't my first. This story is one that my first love told me, to explain why our love didn't work. And now I'm telling it to you, in the exact way it was told to me.

So cosy in close, my Coorie, and I will tell you a story.

1
Cutting Teeth

Once a month my mother, Ash, killed just enough to last until the next. She slunk home triumphant at dusk and hung the bodies in the shed: pheasants, rabbits, the occasional deer in season. The blood trickled under the door and out onto the step. Local cats convened, their tongues rasping in the dark. By morning, the doorstep gleamed white. My mother was a good hunter.

My father, Caleb, worked on a rib boat on Loch Ness. He took tourists out on trips and spun yarns about the things that lurked in the deep waters and dark woods. Some were true, some were not – but what does it matter? There's no such thing as a true story. Caleb memorised Wikipedia entries about power stations and timber, castle architecture and Aleister Crowley. The tourists absorbed his patter like children listening to a bedtime story. They laughed at the funny bits and gasped at the scary bits. My father was a good storyteller.

Each night Ash went into their little kitchen and cooked something that she'd killed, and they ate it together at their little table. Later they'd lie in the dark in their little bed, all chatter and soft laughing, and fall asleep curled like puppies. They weren't my parents yet, but they were in love. Everyone should believe that their parents were in love, even for a while. They were so close to being happy. They had almost everything – but that was not quite enough. For years, it was just the two of them. And then there were three.

My mother brought the wolf home in the season of the hunter's moon: early October, leaf-falling month, the ground burnt and bloody with dead leaves. It was dawn. She was post-hunt, eyes bright, pulse throbbing hard and steady in her wrists.

Caleb came down for breakfast and found his wife standing in the doorway, as if not sure whether to come into the house or run away from it. When she saw him, she came in. The wolf followed. Without thinking, Caleb backed away, putting a chair between himself and the animal. Then he remembered that he was a man, and he stepped forward.

'Is that a wolf?'

'Don't be daft. It's a dog.' She went to the fridge and pulled out a slab of meat. He couldn't tell if it was for his breakfast or the wolf's.

'Looks like a wolf to me.'

'It's a dog. A guard dog. For the house.'

The wolf stood in the corner of the kitchen and watched Caleb warily. His eyes were the same peaty dark as the loch.

'Wolves don't live in houses,' said Caleb. No matter what his wife said, he knew that a wolf was not a dog. Even after she'd cooked the meat and served it with scrambled eggs on two plates, he couldn't

4

shake the feeling that she'd rather have dropped to her knees and eaten the slab raw on the ground.

But no matter what Caleb thought, from that night on the wolf did live in the house. Except for when he lived outside the house – and on those nights, Ash lived outside the house too. She named him Zev. She loved him. And every full moon, he loved her too.

Cold moon, bright as an eye. Together they ran, limbs flexing – and I with them, kept safe beneath skin, curled round as a bean. He already knew about me. He could smell me inside her. He knew long before she did.

leafcrunch – starscent – wetmoss –

I shifted as they ran: wolf to human, human to wolf. Inside her, there was no moon to guide me. I shifted with each fluttering beat of my mother's heart.

moonglow – meatsweet – teethgleam –

One father, two fathers. Two people I could be. Tiny me, shifting wolflike inside my mother.

redtongue – redclaw – tumblelust –

No need for time or patience or restraint. Only food and warmth and love. I was happy there. Softened and sharpened. Complete in my duality.

tumblehome – moondream – sleep.

Perhaps they could have managed, the three of them. But not four.

It was a quiet, bloody day when Ash found out about me. The previous night's hunt was the hunger moon, the February moon, the shortest and the sharpest. Skinning her kill, she lost herself in the texture of meat and sinew. She was happy that day. An unsteady happiness, the way that anything pulled in two directions is easily unbalanced. As she worked, blood pooled in her palms and dried in the creases of her knuckles.

She wiped her free hand dreamily on her apron and caught her breath. She stared down at the red smears. When had she last bled? It had been – two months, three? No, she knew. There was no use in telling herself stories. In her head she listed the next steps: pee on a stick, call Caleb, folic acid. Maternity jeans. Moses basket.

Starscent – meatsweet – moondream.

There in her hanging shed, she placed her knife calmly on the bench. She pressed her hands flat to her belly.

It was a strange day for Caleb too. There was a clan reunion at a hotel on the banks of Loch Ness. Hordes of Canadians and Americans descended on the rib, dressed in their clan tartan, each boasting about their Scaddish heritage. Caleb breathed through his mouth to avoid the reek of mothballs. He swayed with the waves along the rib's aisle, checking the fastenings on the lifejackets, and wondered whether he'd have got more tips if he'd borrowed a mate's wedding kilt. Next time, he thought. I'll remember for next time.

So there was Caleb, loch-spray catching in his eyelashes, legs akimbo on the deck. So there was Ash, hands bloodied from skinning the hunt, hair ponytailed and brow furrowed. Inside my mother, I shifted.

When he got home, she met him at the door holding a piece of plastic the size of her finger. Surprised and tired, he thought it was a toothbrush handle. When he realised what it was he was shocked, and then he was worried, then overjoyed. Later, after they'd eaten dinner at their little table and curled up in their little bed, he was worried again.

'Ash,' he whispered, just loud enough to wake her.

'Yes,' she said, already awake.

'Can we think about Zev?'

'Yes,' she said, already thinking about him.

'I think it's time that someone else had him. You'll be busy enough when the baby comes. You don't need two things to look after. And he needs such long walks. And there's the mud he'll bring in, the germs, it's not good for you. And . . .'

And honestly, it scared him. Most dogs, when people came in the house, would bound forward to get their ears scratched. Even barking, guard dog-style, would be normal enough. But the way it stayed in a corner, dark eyes watching, broad back stretching with each pant of its meaty breath.

'He's not yours, Caleb, he's mine,' she said into the dark. 'I need him. He helps with the hunts. I can't do it without him.'

'I don't know if – love, you can't hunt. Not now.'

'Things don't have to change,' she said.

'Ash. They already have.'

My mother and father were awake for the rest of the night, lying back-to-back. Their bed was not so little any more. The space between them felt wide as the loch.

Ash woke to snores. Layers of tenors and timbres: too many to be just Caleb. He lay burring beside her, mouth tipped open, but from the floor beneath came a chorus of echoes. The room was bright with moon. She wrapped on a housecoat, her limbs tense. She opened her mouth to breathe Zev's name, but he was already beside her, the soft brush of his pelt against her fingertips. Their hearts beat in rhythm. Together they tiptoed downstairs.

Arrayed in the living room was the detritus of the night before. Empty bottles, full ashtrays. A clutch of boys spreadeagled across the floor. Their snoring shook the walls. Ash leaned in to look at the things left in the middle of the coffee table. Chewed-up remnants, blackish with bright scales of bronze. Animal leavings.

The stench caught in her throat, and she turned away with a sound of disgust. Zev's warm tongue lapped at her hand and she wrapped her arms around him, pressing her nose to his dense fur. She closed her eyes and breathed in his musty-dry smell, imagining she was daydreaming on her grandfather's Persian rug, the child Ash still small and safe and entirely herself.

In the bedroom, she woke Caleb. He spoke in yawns. His breath smelled of hops and sickness.

'Me and the boys, we were wetting the baby's head.' He reached out for the swell of her. She took a step back, stumbling as a beer bottle rolled away from her heel.

'Bloody hell, Caleb. You think this is – it's all – no. Just no. I want them out now.'

'Come on. It's early. Let them sleep it off.'

'They shat on the table, Caleb. They chewed up the goldfish and spat it out. I want them gone.'

'Och, they're only playing.' He slid out of bed, scouting in the dimness for his discarded clothes.

'Do you really believe that's how people play? Not even wild animals play like that.'

'What's the big deal? You kill things. Every month you kill more things.'

'We need to eat.'

He stopped foraging around the bedroom and stood before her with his clothes in his arms, underwear creased and skin pasty. She felt the thread of his temper pulling taut.

'We need to eat,' she repeated.

'Killing is killing,' he said.

'Hunting is different, and you know it. I don't bring another animal home, put it in a bowl, feed it every day, and then kill it. No animals do that.'

He threw down his clothes and seized her shoulders. 'Isn't Zev an animal? Doesn't he kill? I've told you it's not safe, ranging round at night with a wild animal, and you just ignore me.'

They faced one another, jaws set. Ash felt her spine lengthen, straighten. The hairs on her arms tingled. A growl hummed deep in her throat. She felt tall enough to smash through the ceiling.

Caleb let his upper lip peel back over his teeth, ready to shout, ready to bite. Ash held his gaze. She did not blink. Caleb let go of her with a sigh and slumped, deflated, down the stairs.

'Party's over, boys,' he called, loud enough that she could hear it through the floor. 'The wife has spoken.'

She wanted to crawl back in bed, bury her face in Zev's warm side. But she was a hunter. Hunters did not run from animals. She tightened her housecoat and went downstairs.

Caleb's boys trailed out of the house, heads slung low, arms apishly slack. She stood by the front door, proud as a stag, ready to slam it shut after the last boy had left.

As they shuffled past they patted her shoulder, pulled her into a loose hug, mumbling sorries. Then she felt the press of a closed fist against her cunt, knuckle to bone. Her breath caught. A clever threat, easy to deny as an accident. All she could see was the backs of their heads as they walked away.

That night, Ash dreamed of Caleb as a wolf, all his boys as wolves; of wolves circling the house and scratching their claws at the windowsills; of being chased by wolves, her bare feet slapping on the wet black roads, the ends of her hair tangling in her mouth; of forests and falling down into the damp mulch of leaves; and finally, as she closed her eyes, ready for the moon-white flash of teeth on her ankle, she woke.

Caleb drove out to the dock. The morning air was spring-fresh, tinged with green. He pushed a cassette into the player. Mixtapes from his teenage years, the paper inserts scrawled with track lists and scratched doodles. The lengths of tape had stretched out over the years. The music through the speakers was slow and soupy. He sang along under his breath, the lyrics so deep in his memory that he didn't know he knew them.

Through the windscreen the loch tried to reflect the grey sky, but only made it darker. The peat in the water meant it was always black – perfect for Nessie to hide in, he'd tell the tourists with a grin. Today it was glass, seeming solid enough to drive out on.

By nine thirty he was halfway through the first tour's patter. The tourists pulled their hoods up against the smirr. They hunched against the rib's sides, gripping the rope handles, peering out across the water. Caleb raised his face to let the soft rain fall on his cheeks.

He told the tourists that he'd been out on the rib almost every day for the past three years. He'd added it up – he'd gone three quarters of the way around the world. The tourists made appreciative noises. When he'd told Ash that, she'd pointed out that he hadn't actually gone anywhere. Just round in circles.

As the rib pulled up beside the glass-bottomed boat, Caleb slowed the engine and reached out his hand – perfectly timed to accept the coffee that Davie on the other boat passed to him. At first he'd done that absent-mindedly, not wanting to stop the rib, but it turned out that the tourists loved it. The smooth lines of his arms, his rough northern hands, his cheeky grin to Davie. It was all part of the story they wanted to tell about Loch Ness when they got home. The picture they coloured in based on his outlines. He didn't even want the coffee now, but he didn't want to lose the giggles when he accepted the cup with a wink.

He settled at the rib's prow and sipped the liquid without tasting it, gunning the engine to move to the next section of the tour. He was thinking about Ash. He was always thinking about Ash. Yes, he'd gone out with the boys and, yes, they'd got a bit rat-arsed. But only to wet the baby's head. And yes, he'd forgotten to lock the door, so they'd come in and carried on the party in the house while he slept. But they'd only done that because he'd left the pub early to get home to Ash and the baby. She couldn't still be angry, could she?

Love was complicated, but it didn't have to be. With him and Ash, it was simple. It always had been. He loved her so much that he would drink the rainwater left in her footprints. She knew it.

He steered the rib over another boat's wake, making it bump and dip rollercoaster-like, letting the tourists leave their stomachs behind. He turned to a stop and launched into the first of a series of elaborate tales about the antics of Aleister Crowley and Jimmy Page at Boleskine House. Black magic and rock music could spark any imagination. The tourists hunched to their knees, trying to keep their balance on the rib's wooden seats while they snapped a photo. All you could see was trees, but it was the story that mattered.

The boys shouldn't have made such a mess. He knew it. But Ash was wrong to call them animals. The wolf – *that* was an animal. It had seemed like a good idea, letting her keep it, but now that he thought about it, he'd only done it to impress the boys. A dog that was mostly a wolf: only a real man would have that in his house, he'd thought. The boys hadn't really cared, but by then Ash was mad for the animal.

But did a real man do things to impress his friends? Peer pressure. Pack mentality. Stupid. He never should have let her bring the thing home. He'd been right: a wolf can't live in a house.

He carried on with his tour patter, but he didn't hear his own words. Instead he was making a resolution. No more following. No more doglike obedience. He was a father. He had to be a man. He'd get rid of the dog by the end of the month.

'It's only a dog, Ash!'

'He's not *only* anything. And he's not even a dog.'

'All the more reason to get rid. It's not safe.'

'I don't care. You're not taking him. We're – he's mine.'

Inside my mother, I squirmed. With each heartbeat I shifted: child, cub, child, cub. Ash grimaced at my motion inside her, peeling her lips back over her teeth.

'What's wrong? Are you okay? Is it the baby?'

'I'm fine, Caleb. It's my baby.'

My father laughed. It came out like a protest. 'Ours, you mean. The baby is ours.'

'Well, it's not inside you, is it?'

In the silence that followed, I heard much. I heard decisions being made for me. I heard lives constricting and contracting. I heard something end.

You might wonder how I know all this. How I could hear and see things before I had ears and eyes. I'm telling you this story, and I know it's true as much as anything is true. All my life I have been wild. I have tried to let my brain and my heart choose, but my mouth, salivating and unruly, has decided for me. I always eat the first and last bites of food, no matter whose plates they are on. Leather shoes squeeze my feet to shuffles. My teeth are so sharp they cut my tongue. Something is missing in me. Something has been lost. I know that I was once a wolf – and then I was not.

'This is our baby, Ash,' said my father. 'I am going to do what is best. For now and for always, I will do everything I can to keep our baby safe. And until the baby comes out, that means doing everything I can to keep you safe too.'

Bright night, May light, milk moon. They ran. Their paws were damp with blood.

nightgrin – eyegleam – tonguesoft –

Inside her, I was so close to being happy. So close to being outside her.

woodleap – mossbed – moonkiss –

Already my fingers were separate, the buds of my incisors formed, the fists of my lungs getting ready to open.

mouthslip – teethnip – tonguewet –

But in the end, we can only be one person.

tumblehome – moondream – sleep, sleep, sleep.

Ash woke to growls. She slid clumsily out of her dreams, eyes gummed. She flexed her feet and dirt flaked onto the bedsheets.

The room was dark. She saw a shadow move against the shadows. The air hummed with sound. She didn't want to see what she was seeing.

Zev, hunched on Caleb's sleeping chest. Teeth bared over his pale stubbled throat. Jaw ready to snap.

Her heart choked up her throat. She slithered to the ground and hissed Zev's name. Still, the growls. Still, the shadow. She lunged for him, arms around his rough-furred centre, and knocked him away. His bones landed with a thud. The growls turned to a yelp, a series of cries. She lifted her bare foot to kick him out of the room – but already he'd skittered out, jaw shut tight.

She hunched in the corner, heart choking. She couldn't. He couldn't. It wasn't.

When she was calm, she woke Caleb. She asked him to take Zev away, right now, in the night, so she could start the next day without him. Fall asleep as one person, wake up as another.

'Please, Caleb,' she said. 'Please.' She held him tight, feeling the press of their child, so that he would not ask why.

Caleb did not need much convincing. He took Zev hunting. He left the body out in the woods for the foxes to eat.

Ash salted hunks of venison, ready to cure. Remnants of deer, of rabbit, of pheasant. She'd have to make it last. She'd make the meat into prosciutto, the furs into gloves, the feathers into hats. With the money she would buy a rib and tour with Caleb in pairs when the baby came. This dying moon marked the end of her hunts.

There are times when we are more than one person. With me inside her, my mother held two people in her one skin. I too was two, a shifting wolfchild in the moon of her belly. But we must always choose. My mother tried not to choose; tried to be two people in one seamless skin. And for a while, she managed it. But it couldn't last. If there was a way for her to be a hunter and a mother, she could not find it. This, this she could do: the paired tour, man and woman, the two of them. And baby makes three. Complete. The tourists would go batshit. They'd want to take her photo, legs akimbo on the rib, her baby burbling in its sling, against the backdrop of peaty water and shadowed trees. She'd better get a haircut. Maybe a new jacket.

With bare hands she sleeve-pulled the empty rabbit pelt, putting the fur on the inside and the flesh on the outside. After Caleb had taken Zev away, she'd fallen back into an uneasy sleep. She'd dreamed again of Caleb as a wolf, all his boys as wolves; of being chased, and bare feet, and forests and falling down – but instead of the white flash of teeth on her ankle, she had been the teeth. She had turned, mid-chase, and opened her jaws wide enough to devour Caleb and all his dogs in a single bite.

Was it normal to fear your dreams? To fear yourself? But Zev was gone. Just like that, adopted out to a new home. Another fool who thought a wolf could live in a house. Surely that part of her could be given away as easily. She was a woman, and she had a man. It was enough. She would make it be enough. She'd made her choice.

In the end we can wear only one skin, speak with only one tongue. We choose one, and the other is lost. Ash dunked the rabbit pelt in cold water, ensuring every trace of blood was gone. She held it submerged until the cold-water burn in her hands faded to numbness.

Liska:

Hush, hush, don't fidget. Your mama is sleeping. It's just us now, hiding in the night-time. Hush, I tell you! Let your mama sleep while your other mama talks to you. The dark brings stories, and I want to share one.

You can't see it yet, but there's a lighthouse nearby. Every minute its steady beam sweeps through our window and lights up the room. It lights up this table beside the bed, and this horrible creature upon it. You can't imagine ugliness yet, so trust when I say it's terribly, terribly ugly. It's called a troll, and your mama only allows one inside the house, she hates them so. Every time I go back to Norway I leave a little of my old self there – but in return I bring back a troll. Another ugly, misshapen thing carved from local wood. I line them up on the doorstep – your mama prefers that, for them to be outside. She doesn't like all the reminders of the parts of myself I leave behind. Oh, not that the old versions of me are foul, rotten, filthy with sin – or anyhow, no more so than anyone else. We all do a little bit of wrong. You'll see that soon.

But your mama lets me bring just one troll inside, because she knows as well as I do that our pasts can also be protection. A scar

17

shows you survived. A nightmare shows you what you love too much to lose. And here's the thing about trolls: the uglier, the better. Ugliness is not to be feared. It's beauty that hides the danger.

And that brings me to my story. My own mama told me it when I was much bigger a thing than you are now. I wish she'd told me sooner, so I could have known the wonders and dangers of it. That is why I am telling you these stories. I know that you'll make your mistakes, learn your lessons. But I hope that these stories will save you a few. We all make them, but you don't have to make all of them.

Are you sitting comfortably? I can't feel you, so I will have to trust.

2
The Keep

We started with a ring. We thought she would like that. When she opened the drawer and saw the ring there, reclining gleamingly on a hank of pink silk, her face opened up sunny-joyful. We knew that she thought it was from him. That couldn't be helped.

She put it straight onto her finger. We watched her toy cattish with it for the rest of the day, twisting it to and fro as she swooned and hummed around the caravan. When she'd first arrived she'd moved slyfoot, placed teacups down with fretting care, each step tightroping. We knew why. When we'd first arrived, we'd seen the way the little tin caravan sat high in the tree, bound to the thick oak branches, hung flimsy-like over a fast-flowing burn. We'd all moved slyfoot then too, at first. We had not wanted to make the caravan fall clatter-crash out of the tree. But soon we settled, just as she was settled, and her steps fell hard as hail. That was when we crept out of our hiding places.

To and fro, to and fro she twisted the ring. She cleaned in time with her songs, finding pretty nooks for all the things that needed tidied away. A pint of milk, a pink slinking nightgown, a dustpan, a pair of toothbrushes. The caravan was a labyrinth of hidings: drawers and cupboards and little sneaky nooks. Finally she felt the words spark scratchy on her skin. She frowned, pulling off the ring to peer at its innards. *Until I die*. She rubbed where the etched words had caught her. If we had had breath, we would have held it.

We watched her frown a realisation, then release it in fear of wrinkles. We knew as well as she did that he would not stand for wrinkles. Perhaps the ring was not a gift from him after all. Perhaps she'd stumbled on the remnants of old loves. But whose? *Until I die* – and he was still alive.

She tried to open the drawer and hide the ring. But that drawer would not open again today. She tugged and she coaxed, but the drawer stuck fast. Finally she hid the ring in her face cream, dropping it in and shaking the little pot until it was submerged. We watched as she opened and opened and opened the bathroom cupboards until she found one the perfect size, its edges kissing the face cream pot as she slid it in. Such tininess in the caravan, but always somewhere to be secret.

When he came home, she greeted him with neat kisses. We hid in the smallest cupboard and listened. There was no talk of gifts. Her finger was swollen where the words had scratched, but he did not notice. Outside the caravan, the rain shushed and the wind throbbed and the moon blinked bright. Inside, time stopped. The chattering burn stole all sound; the spreading leaves took all sight.

After dinner, he used his petty magic to transform the couch into their bed. They lay together. We wished that we still had hands, so that we could cover our ears.

The next day, after he had left, we tried again. A hair ribbon. Plush velvet, thick as wolf-fur, red as a heart. She found it while trying drawers in search of washing-up gloves. She forgot about the dishes and reached for the ribbon. It curled lovingly into her hand, and with a turn she bumped the drawer shut with her hip. She pulled back her conker-shining curls with one hand, the other ribbon-busy.

But – a tickle on her fingersides. She stopped and peered. Three hairs twist-tangled in the ribbon, ever so long and ever so blonde. We watched her look at the hairs. We watched her stroke the blood-red ribbon. We watched her fingers come away wet. With a cry she dropped the ribbon and kicked it away from her.

She didn't try to open the drawer again this time. She knotted and knotted and knotted the ribbon and she opened her underwear drawer and pushed it right to the corner, covering it up with her fripperies and frills.

When he came home they ate in silence. Her fingertips were stained red. They went to bed, and we had no need of covering our ears. In the darkness we heard the click-clack of her thoughts.

We watched her open the drawer four more times in four more days. We left her a silken negligee delicate as mothwings, a pair of stockings twisted garrotte-thin, eyelashes faded grey and crumbling, painted fingernails with fleshly scraps caught at their bases. And on the seventh day, we left her a heart.

We watched her open the drawer as though she were looking into a lion's mouth. She'd turned slyfoot again. Despite the labyrinthing, she was running out of places to hide our things. She pulled back when she saw the heart, enthroned in the drawer among a scatter of dried roses. It shivered in a single beat. She leaned in. Perhaps she thought it was a kitten, butter-soft and full of mewls. Perhaps all these gifts were from him after all.

We watched her lift out the heart. She held it in her hands. She squeezed it. Hard. The flesh bulged around her fingers. Of course she did not think it was a kitten. Now we understood her thoughts and her insides as if her skin were made of glass.

He'd taken a caravan, a portable shelter, ordinary as dirt – he'd taken it and magicked it into a labyrinth for girls, a make-believe home the size of eight coffins lashed together. Some girls escaped, but we didn't. We ignored the signs, or the signs weren't there. We'd got lost and we'd never been found. Our tangles of hair, our bright scraps of frock: tossed up into the trees, to be worked into birds' nests. Our straight white bones and our tender mauve organs: dropped down into the burn, carried out to sea. He thought that was the end of us.

She spoke to us then. She told how he had found her. Rescued her. Claimed her. Made her see that the world was cold and dark and hard and empty – but with him, life would be delicious, abundant. He'd put his hands over her eyes, and when he took them away she saw differently. The happenings before him were too hard to focus on, furled and dark like sun-damaged film. All she could see was his face.

We know, we cried, though she could not hear. We all knew his face. It was the last thing we'd seen. We shouted that it would be the last thing she'd see too. He'd tear out her heart just so he could hold it in his hands. He'd throw the remnants of her to the trees and the sea.

Some of them ran long before reaching the heart. Some of them ignored its urgent throb, staying until they couldn't leave. But for her, this was enough. She dropped the heart. With her bloodied hands, she tore open the door. She ran away.

We knew she wouldn't be back. We slipped back into the littlest cupboards and waited for him to come back to his crowded, empty home.

Ruth:

You know something, my Coorie? I'm promising you much with these stories. Every story ever told is a promise: stick with me and I'll tell you some truths. Clear directions, relatable characters: a breadcrumb trail, each part linking from the one before to the one after. And I want life to be like that for you. I want your life to make sense. If I had three wishes, I'd wish them all on that.

But life is not a fairy tale. It's brighter and darker, longer and briefer, duller and more magical. It's full of contradictions, but one thing it's not is neat.

I could tell you a story about how your other mother and I came to this tiny sea-blown house – about how our lives slowly, inevitably formed us into the people who would one day make a life here. She'll be at the radio station all day, so I can tell you anything I like. It's just you and me, and the gulls and the sea.

But that story would be a lie. It's putting sense where there was no sense. There's no single reason we decided to make a baby and move north. There's no simple event-and-consequence that made us want to make ourselves anew in the middle of nowhere. We did it, and it's done, and here we are. Whatever comes next for us all will seem obvious too, but I have no idea what that will be – and if I can't predict it now, can I honestly say that it's the obvious next step? There's no way to sum up a complex, messy, contradictory person in a sentence – and yet each time we tell a story, that's exactly what we try to do. We try to turn our lives into stories so that they make sense, because we think that stories must make sense.

When I was little, I thought that everyone's past was a series of steps, like a board game. I know now that it's not so simple. Real life is beautiful because it isn't neat. Are you ready, Coorie? The sea is quiet. The birds float, wings tucked, bobbing on the waves. The sun has come out for you.

Now I'm going to tell you a story that isn't a story, because it's true.

3
Ex-

Ex-brother

When I was ten years old, I found out that my dad was not my dad. My real dad was some guy I'd never met, a bricklayer from Mull who'd met my mum in a nightclub in town one Easter weekend. That was enough, the dad thing, but it turned out that he also had another kid. Rosabeth. Born two years before me. She lived with her dad, who was also my dad, because her mum had run off.

I know what people will be thinking – she's the reason my real dad didn't stay with my mum. He already had a child and didn't want another, or he already had enough responsibility, or he was scared my mum would run off and leave him a double-single dad. I'm going to stop everyone before they start, because that's not what this is about.

I get it. Stories need sense. Connection, logic, motivation. 'He did this later because this happened to him earlier.' But not here. I want to say right now, upfront, that this isn't a nice and neat and psychologically satisfying story. Because it's not a story. It's my life. These things happened, and none of them explains any of the other. Sometimes things just happen.

The thing about Rosabeth was, even though she was born two years before me, she wasn't two years older than me. I was ten, and she was eight, and she would always be eight because she was dead. By the time I found out that I was a brother, I wasn't one any more.

I didn't meet up with my dad then. The only reason I found out about him was that I'd been nosing through Mum's Boring Folder, trying to find something with her signature to copy it on a teacher's letter. There was a birth certificate, okay, and it wasn't my dad's name under 'Father'. Well, he was my dad, but – you know what I mean. When my mum got home I threw the birth certificate at her and had a proper tantrum. I was such a brat when I was a kid. Then she told me the whole story, which is partly how I know that stories are all bullshit. The story was neat and logical and I hated it.

Anyway, then she showed me the letters, where she'd hidden them in the airing cupboard under the spare duvet. She'd had a letter from him every year since I was born. Then for the past four years it had doubled: one on my birthday and one on Rosabeth's deathday. He never talked about Rosabeth in the letters, except once to say that she'd died. He never talked about anything in particular. But I liked them – the jags of his Ts and Js, the way the lines of words slanted up to the right more and more so that by the end of the letter they were diagonal. I put the letters back in the airing cupboard, because that's where they belonged. I didn't need them in my room or under my pillow or anything.

That was it, really. I found out that my dad wasn't my dad, and for a while I hated him and my mum, and then I went back to school and to my karate class and to my best mate's house. I got on with things, like you do. Later, I know that people are going to think that

Rosabeth being dead, or my dad not being my dad, was the reason that other things happened. But remember what I said. Sometimes things just happen.

Ex-victim

There's a film called *Lolita*, and it's really sad and creepy. Things happen to her, and it's extra sad and creepy because she can't do anything about it. Well, it's not like that for boys. Things don't happen to boys because boys make things happen. Poor wee Lolita: only thirteen, and she gets used and abused by an old perv. But with boys, when they're thirteen, it's exciting because it's an older woman and not a man.

Older women can teach a boy things, sexual and emotional and life-type things. It's an important experience for any boy. Most boys make it happen when they're about fifteen, and that's what makes them men. Most of them don't talk about it, though, because it would be disrespectful to the woman and she might get in trouble if people misunderstood. I made it happen a bit earlier than most boys because I'm more mature and I could handle it. I was definitely ready at twelve, but Mrs – my lover, I mean – she wanted to wait for me to come to her. That's how it works: the woman sits still and looks seductive, and the man comes over and seduces her. Which is what I did.

At first we actually did the tutoring, properly and not just pre-tending. She'd set me geography questions, true/false and multiple choice and essays. Her perfume wasn't like the girls at school – they smell like vanilla and chocolate, sweet things. She smelled low and rich. Musky, but good. She'd get me a Coke and watch while I drank it. She'd let the strap of her dress slip off her shoulder, so the curve of her breast showed. I didn't notice at first because I was doing the questions.

And then one day – See, no. I'm not doing this. I'm making it seem like a story, beginning-middle-end, and it wasn't like that. It's true that Mrs – that she was my tutor, and that at first she wasn't my lover and then later she was. Then even later a few people found out, and she had to leave the school so there wouldn't be a scandal and a court case, which was really unfair because I wanted it. That whole thing about me being groomed, and her taking advantage, and me being too traumatised to tell the truth – that was a stupid story that my mum and dad had to tell themselves. I've read that shit in the papers too, about other people. Beautiful nymphet boys with their tousled blonde hair and their little red mouths. Poor, poor boys. I believed it then. Now I see it was all probably made up. Those were old photos in the papers, and by the time it happened they were men, and they wanted it.

It didn't *happen to* me. I made it happen. So how could I be a victim, if I wanted it?

Ex-missing person

I ran away with my dad when I was fifteen. My real dad, I mean. I'd met him by this point – didn't I mention that? See, if this was a story I'd have to have mentioned that before.

He was meant to have me for the weekend. We were going to Alton Towers. But on the Wednesday before, there he was at the school gates. He looked uncomfortable, a bit shifty, as if – No. I'm doing it again. I didn't even notice how he looked because I was so happy to see him. He might have been yodelling the national anthem and doing a jig for all I can remember.

We got in his car and drove to the border as if we were going to Alton Towers. I don't think I even asked him where we were going. I didn't care. He'd brought me a change of clothes – jeans and a hoodie, cool brands, new ones with the tags still on. The radio was up loud and he was smoking out of the window. We stopped for lunch at a Little Chef. My chips were soggy.

Look – none of this matters. I'm trying to make it a story for everyone who'll hear it and I shouldn't do that, it's a bad habit I'm trying to break. What matters is that I was never missing. I always knew where I was. My dad always knew where I was. We were right there in the car together. So how could I be missing, if two people knew my exact whereabouts at all times? My mum and my other dad didn't know, and that's where the fuss came from. It might be nice for them to think that usually they always know where I am – for them to have a picture, a neat mental photograph, at any time of the day or night. But it's made up. They never know exactly where I am.

Say my timetable is Maths, so they close their eyes and imagine me at a middle desk, chewing my pen, frowning at fractions. Ahhh, look at the wee boy, doing his maths. Then they can open their eyes and get on with sending emails or sneakily playing games on their phones or nodding off in meetings or whatever they do. But maybe I'm not there at all. Maybe I've gone to the loo, or the teacher's off sick so we're in a different classroom. Maybe my timetable was suddenly changed so I'm not in Maths at all, I'm in German. Or I've got a free period now and I've gone into town to look at the shops. What I mean is, they don't know where I am. They never really know. They like to pretend that they do.

It was only when we'd passed the Alton Towers signs that I said to Dad. I thought he'd just missed the sign because he was too busy driving or flicking ash out of the window. He just mumbled something back. I wasn't worried or anything – why would I be? He's my dad. I noticed then that he had a little picture of a girl tacked up on the dashboard, over the speedometer. I knew it was Rosabeth because she looked a bit like me. She was cute. She was mid-action, her mouth in a wonky smile, trying to stick out her tongue. She was wearing a sundress and holding an ice-cream that was melting down the cone and onto her hand in merging pink lines. It must have been taken somewhere hot.

I know what people will be doing. They'll be trying to make this into a story. They'll be thinking that my dad stole me because he'd lost his daughter. One child lost, one child taken. Well, I'll say this: he'd decided that we'd all be together years ago, long before Rosabeth died. So everyone should stop making this a story. He'd planned to take both of us to a better life, he told me, so we could all live happily ever after. Down to Dover, then across to Calais, and then the whole of Europe was our oyster. That's a good story, right? But that's why it was bullshit.

And then – I don't know. My dad changed his mind. It was dark by then, and if I'd thought about it I'd have known that my mum and other dad had reported me missing. Except that I hadn't thought

32

about them at all. I never really thought about them when they weren't there.

So we were at the Dover port, lights glinting off the inky sea, the thunder-boom of the ferries shifting. We were almost at the front of the queue and it was our turn to drive onto the ferry. Instead of going forward my dad swung the car around, slipping fast and messy between the lines of cars all tooting their horns. He turned away from the port and took me home. I don't remember us speaking for the rest of the drive back to Scotland. It would be neat to say that I never saw him for the rest of my life after that night, wouldn't it? But I'm not dead yet, so I can't say what will happen for the rest of my life.

I know everyone will want to know why he did it. Why he did all of it. They'll want logic and character motivation. Well, tough.

Ex-boyfriend

Eden never said I was her boyfriend. We were seventeen, fuck – we were adults. Why would we bother with stupid words like that? It didn't even matter. We were so in love, and everyone could see it. It didn't matter what we called it.

We'd get burgers in town or see a film or skive classes and walk through the park. We'd talk about our futures. Eden was good at futures. She told me about how we were going to get married – none of that conformist shit with diamond rings and seating plans, obviously. We'd elope to Hawaii and write our own vows and get married barefoot on the beach. She'd wear a white bikini and I'd carve her a wedding ring out of the bones of a fish I'd caught. It would be perfect.

There were other futures too. We'd live in a cottage with roses around the door. We'd have two kids: twins, a boy and a girl, called River and Rain. We'd make shitloads of money in finance and then cash it all in and live on a boat. We'd rescue puppies. We'd never get sick or old. We'd be together forever.

And then – well. The future is a story we tell ourselves, and 'perfect' is the biggest story of all. I was never her boyfriend so I never had to be her ex-boyfriend, and worry about all the shitty baggage that went with that. I don't need that. I'm a lone wolf, an easy rider. That's the true story – Oh, fuck it, I'm doing it again. There's no story. She never called me her boyfriend, and that's all.

Why didn't we work out? We just didn't. We loved each other more than anyone has ever loved. Then one day she didn't love me anymore.

I wanted to know why, like everyone will want to know why. Eden told her friends that she was bored of me. She told her parents that I wasn't serious enough about my future. She told her sister that I didn't appreciate her. She told me that we were better as friends – that I knew her better than anyone – that I was her Best Friend and always would be – that our future was friends, going out for dinner at weekends and sharing love advice and maybe one day adopting brother-and-sister puppies.

People always have to make things into stories so they're easier. So they can tell them to other people, to get sympathy or a laugh, to try to explain themselves. 'I only did this because this happened to me.' But life isn't like that.

34

Ex-father

The thing about Eden is that she was really close with her mum and her sister, so she didn't need me to go with her to get the operation. She didn't even tell me about it until after. The stomach cramps had mostly gone by then, but she had to wear this big padded nappy thing, like incontinence pants for old people. That's why she didn't want me to come round, so I wouldn't see the nappy thing bulking out her skinny jeans. It looked funny, she said, and she didn't want me to see. She said it was funny but she was crying a bit too, and I didn't know whether to laugh or cry either.

And, honestly, this is the one where I stumble a bit. She didn't do it because we'd broken up, but maybe if we hadn't . . . and she didn't break up with me because she already knew, but maybe if she did know . . . and it wasn't the reason why, she didn't get this baby-fear and suddenly think, Fuck, I don't want to have kids with this guy, I'd better . . . And it wasn't even a baby, she said, just some cells and redness.

By the time I found out I was a dad – No. I'm not going to say that. If I say that, everyone will remember the other bit I said at the beginning, and they'll think they're connected. They're not. They're fucking not. I was never going to call that girl-baby Rosabeth. That would be stupid and sick. I didn't even know her. Not Rosabeth, and not the ball of cells, and not really Eden if I'm honest. But she didn't know me either. If she did, she wouldn't have been able to walk away like that. If she knew me, she'd love me. Everyone does. My dad loved me so much he went to prison for stealing me. Mrs – my lover, she lost her job for loving me. Not that those things are connected. They're just other things that happened.

I know everyone hearing this will still want answers. But look at your life. You probably think it's pretty logical. You do things that make sense, right? You might be a mystery wrapped in an enigma, but still, you don't do things for no reason. Given the specifics of your life, everything you do is what any sane, intelligent person would do in the same situation.

You vote right because this country is going to shit. You vote left because this country is going to shit. You're a nurse because your granny was a nurse. You have trust issues because your mum left you on a doorstep. You want lots of kids because you were an only child. You want lots of kids because you had a big family. You hate dogs because a dog once bit you. You became a painter because you had night-terrors. You failed your exams because your parents were divorcing.

Because, because, because. I hate that fucking word.

It's only after that fact that we trace the lines, join dots between things, skip over anything that doesn't fit. We make stories to account for everything that's happened. It's nice to think the world makes sense. It's nice to think that you make sense. But sometimes things just happen.

Liska:

Hello my little sweetmeat, my tiny clam, my hermit crab. I've got a tale for you, my tiny whelk, my fattening mollusc.

I brought you something from the seashore. Look, a mermaid's purse. Wait, wait, and in a moment the lighthouse beam will sweep through the room. Ah! There! Yes, I know you can't see yet. But not to fret, I'll keep it here for you. For now, your mama sleeps, and it's time for a story.

I brought you this mermaid's purse because it reminded me of you. You're a flickering silver minnow, a tiny bright anemone. Your mama is making you and in return you feed from her, floating in your blood-fed sac. She's everything to me, but when I gave her my heart, I kept some back for you. I can't wait to give you it: a red pulse, the last of my love. I haven't even met you, and I love you. You are my favourite parasite, and you can feed off me until you are full. I would turn myself inside out for you. I'd build a shelter from my bones to keep you warm. I'd give you my eyes if you thought they'd taste sweet. But that sort of love – do you understand that we can't always love that way? We only have two eyes to give. Organs and bones don't grow back. A parasite can kill.

One day you will love. I can't tell you how, and I wouldn't. What do I know? What do any of us know? But this isn't my story. This is the story of my little sister, Mirren. It's a nasty tale, and no pretty sugar-dusting can change that. But Mirren told me it so I could learn from it, and I want you to learn too. I want you to know when to give, and when to take. I want you to know how to make your own magic. Lie still and open up your tiny ears.

4
The Perfect Wife

May

Once upon a time there was a woman who loved her husband. She loved him completely, blindly, consumingly, the way a woman should. She'd had lovers before she met her husband, but with them she'd been distant, preoccupied, already full up with her work and her life and her own opinions and beliefs and thoughts. But this time she was going to get it right. This time she had cleared out a space inside her the exact size of her husband. For him, she would be as beautiful and empty as the rosy pearlised shells she saw on the beach. For him, she would be perfect.

She woke before dawn to paint on a better version of her face: lips pinkened, eyelashes lengthened, blemishes hidden. She brushed her hair a hundred times until it gleamed like spun gold. She threw her sleep-rumpled nightgown into the wash, then pulled on a freshly-ironed one. She crept back into bed as her husband awoke.

'Morning, sleepyhead,' he said. 'Gorgeous as always. Look at me, all crusty eyes and stubble, and you're a wee angel. A natural beauty.'

She smiled. She wanted to be beautiful the way that he wanted her to be beautiful. She timed it so she was inhaling his exhalations, breathing his sleep-sour breath, pulling him into her lungs. She slid below the covers and took him in her mouth, gently and then firmly.

Afterwards she went into the kitchen, drank a glass of water, and started his breakfast. He stumbled in as she was sliding the bacon and eggs from the pan to the plate. He kissed the top of her head and took his place at the head of the table.

'Only two more nights,' he said through a mouthful of buttered toast. 'Then I'm away. Will you be alright?'

'I love you,' she said. And it was true. She knew that he loved her too. He'd kill tigers for her, if tigers were, for some reason, to convene on their small Scottish fishing village.

'I know you do,' he said. 'I know. And it's not for long. I'll be one month on, one month off. That's good, isn't it? We'll have plenty time together when I'm home. Sure you won't get bored and run off?'

She frowned. 'I love you.'

'Oh, Mirren! I know. But it's a lonely life. Most wives, they have kids or jobs to keep them busy while their men are away. Will you look for something while I'm gone? Maybe helping out at the school, or in the shop? I bet they'd be glad to have you.'

She smiled at her husband. She would do whatever he wanted, whenever he wanted, the way a woman should. He said he had to leave, to work out at sea. But she knew that he'd never leave her, not even for a moment. Because she loved him, she couldn't bear the thought of ever going away from him, and so he could never go away from her either.

But two days later, he did.

June

Once a woman had love. For some people, their love is not enough. No matter how much they try to love, they never feel quite full. They always know that something is missing – a gnawing need, a gap that their love can't fill.

But not for this woman. Her love was too much. It filled up the space she had made for it, but it did not stop. Her love expanded her chest and pressed at the backs of her eyes. Her love swelled her legs and split the bases of her fingernails. Her love grew and grew until she was ready to burst.

Her husband was gone and it was the longest day of the year, which was worse than the longest night. The pale light itched. It was relentless. If night could only come, that meant the day would be over, and she was a little closer to having her husband again. But it was just this day, this endless day. She wished for the hush of night, the velvety dark. Without her husband, there could be no rest. Love bloated her, ballooned her weightless to the pale sky.

She slipped from her lonely bed, nightgown rumpled from her lack of sleep. No need for pinkened lips or spun-gold hair without her husband there. He was at sea, so she followed him. Barefoot through the marram grass. Quick steps across the sand. Ankles in the shallows, feet numb within minutes. Soft thrusts of warmth when she stood on sharp stones and the blood pulsed out. She waded, feeling the sway and tug of the water at her thighs, her hips, her chest, her throat. Her feet left the seabed.

'Oy! What you doing? It's no swimming here.'

She turned back towards the shore, towards the shouts – but the hush, the soothe of the waves – she turned away. The water tickled her jaw.

'Come ashore! There's an undertow. You'll drown, you idiot!'

A splash. She tipped her head away from the relentless sky, down into the water. She floated. The waves would carry her to her husband.

Then the pressure of fingers on her wrist. A yank on her arm, jerking its socket. Her face ripped from the sea.

A man. With his arm around her, his rough hand under her chin, pulling against the waves, pulling her away. A man who was not her husband.

He dropped her on the damp sand, his breath coming in gasps. She turned her head to the side and coughed out seawater.

'Are you bloody mental? It's dangerous! You could have died.'

She coughed again, her throat raw. She lay back on the sand. She got ready to feel her love expanding, pressing at her eyelids, stretching her skin. Without the pressure of the water to hold her, she would surely float up into the sky.

But something was wrong. She was solid. She was heavy, weighted. She felt the tiny dents of stones pressing into her skin.

'I know you. It's Mirren, right? From the next farm over? Your husband's on the rigs. Is he at home just now? Shall I call him?'

The man who was not her husband leaned over her, peering at her face. She turned her head to the side, to better concentrate on the feeling of the beach beneath her – and she saw the image etched onto his wrist.

An anchor. She reached out to touch it. An anchor, to keep her grounded.

She tried to speak, but the words were too rough. They scraped the sides of her throat. Then she thought of the words she wanted to say to her husband, and they slid out as slick as melting ice: 'I love you.'

The man who was not her husband laughed, then frowned. 'Shit, Mirren. Are you okay? Do you need to go to the hospital? You seem . . .'

She wrapped her fingers around his wrist, pressing her palm to the anchor. For the first time since her husband had left, she could touch the ground. Her back, her thighs, her heels: all of it weighed on the earth. She was safe. She was balanced.

'Listen, I'm going to call the doctor. You seem a bit spacey, you know? Let me go and get my phone – it's at the house, it's just over the hill there, I'll be back in a minute.'

The shadow of him pulled away. Above her the sky loomed, white and wide. She felt herself falling into it. She reached for the only solid thing she knew.

'Whoa! Okay. Don't grab me, it's okay. I won't go. But I can't call the doc, and you don't seem quite right, so –'

'I love you. I love you.'

She reached for him: her saviour, her anchor. Her husband.

He started to laugh, but stopped. He started to frown, but stopped.

'What do you – why are you saying that?'

She reached for him and pulled him close. The weight of him on her body. The warmth. The breath. She was anchored.

'Mirren, come on now. You're shivering. We can't.'

She pressed kisses to his forehead, his cheek, his throat.

'Or is it – do you just want me to warm you? In a, like, in a medical way? Is that it?' His breath came fast. His voice dropped low.

'We can't,' he murmured, as she pulled down his jeans, pulled up her dress. 'We can't,' as she pressed him inside her.

Her ears filled with the sounds of waves. She smelled saltwater. She looked up into her husband's face. She closed her eyes and heard his voice in her head: *I love you.*

July

Once a woman lived without her husband. The day was clear and bright. She'd been awake since before dawn. Her husband was coming home today. The bed was warm, the blankets heaped mountain-like, the cat curled into a comma at the foot of it. The longer she stayed in bed, the shorter the day she would have to endure before she saw him. She hated the length of empty days.

The postman clattered the letterbox. She did not move; she did not care what the letters said. There was no use in words if they were not from her husband's lips.

Hours passed. She was too hot; she pushed the blankets away. A helicopter burred overhead. The neighbour's dog barked. A tractor coughed to life. She was too cold; she pulled the blankets back.

Then: footsteps on the path. Her husband! She jumped out of bed so fast that she tripped over the cat. Her elbow throbbed where it met the floor. The front door swung open. Her husband's voice from the hall.

'Did you miss me, little mermaid?'

She made it out of the bedroom before her legs lost their bones. She collapsed into her husband's arms.

'Whoa, Mirren! Watch yourself; you nearly bumped your wee bonce there. Don't cry! I'm happy to see you too. I've got you, my love. Oh, don't cry now. I've got you. What is it, hey? What's wrong?'

Her throat had closed. She pressed her face into her husband's shoulder, mouthing the words even though he couldn't hear them.

I love you. I love you. I love you.

Now that her husband was home, home was the world. There was no sea. There was no shore. There was only this: the four walls around the two of them.

She neatened the bed, made fish stew for dinner, sliced a rough loaf onto two plates. Her cheeks ached from smiling.

Her husband watched her as she moved around the world of their home. She could feel his soft gaze on her. It made her heart feel solid and steady inside her, and she moved to its rhythm. Beat-pause, beat-pause, beat.

'You want tea, love?'

She nodded. Her husband picked up the kettle and went to fill it. He leaned across the sink to peer out of the window, one hand holding the kettle, one palm digging into the windowsill.

'What's all this stuff in the yard? Are you trying to open a junk shop or something? Is it an art project?'

She practised replies in her head as she stirred the pot of stew. It was a palace, it was a home, it was a way to make him stay. None of it sounded quite right, so she didn't say any of it.

Her husband clicked on the kettle. She leaned over the pot, scooping hot liquid onto a spoon to taste it.

'Well, whatever it is, I'm glad. It's good that you're working on something.' He tipped loose leaves into the teapot. He stepped behind her, resting his hands on her shoulders. 'I worry, Mirren. I didn't like being away for so long. I never like going away. I hate leaving you.'

She told him then. With the steam from the pan condensing on her upper lip, with the kettle exhaling on the counter, with his sweetly calloused hands resting on her shoulders. She told him that she loved him so much that she couldn't contain her love. She told him that she couldn't stand to be without his love, not even for a day. She told him that she loved him so much, she had to have two husbands, so that she never had to be without one.

Or she tried to tell him. Or she thought about telling him. Or she just opened her mouth and closed it again. She knew the pressure of words on her ears, and she knew that she hadn't spoken aloud.

The kettle reached its boil, rocking on its base. Her husband's hands left her shoulders. Without the weight holding her, she felt dizzy. Her lungs were balloons, her skull swollen full of air. She felt her feet leave the ground. She was unanchored, unmoored, unmanned.

She turned to her husband and wrapped his arms around her shoulders, leaving the pan to overboil. It didn't matter. Nothing mattered except that her husband was here.

August

Once there lived a woman who had two husbands. In the evenings she walked alone on the shore, between her husbands. She walked with one foot in the sand, one foot in the sea. The air carried woodsmoke; the breeze shifted and brought her saltwater. The two scents of her husbands.

That particular evening the high tide had brought her blue china shards, brass grates tangled with rope, the legs of plastic toys. She collected up these things because they were pieces of her husband's sea-palace. He had to go there but she could not go with him, so he sent her these tokens. She would collect the pieces and rebuild the palace for him – not at sea, but on land. She would do this because he was her husband. She would do this because she wanted her husband to be here with her. Not in the sea-palace. Not where she was not.

With a canvas bag on each arm, she cleared the sand. After an hour she was perfectly balanced, each arm weighed down with debris. Dining sets and tables and fireplaces and rope-swings, all in pieces, deconstructed, ready for her to remake.

Bags full, she turned towards home. Her husband would be waiting there for her. The late-evening sand cooled her feet while the marram grass scratched her ankles. She paused.

An empty Campbell's Cream of Chicken Soup tin made a slow, stumbling walk out of the grass, towards the sea. Behind it followed a doll head and a jam jar. If she looked closely, she could see the crabs' legs skittering away underneath. If they weren't careful, someone would lift up that soup tin and that doll head and that jam jar and have themselves a lovely crab dinner. She hefted her bags and continued home. Silly crabs! Imagine thinking that you could take shelter anywhere. Shelters were built, not found.

Home was a lamplit cottage at the end of a winding bramble-lined path. It was whitewashed and slate-roofed and it had fat pink flowers framing the front door to welcome visitors. She approached instead across the fields, each step taking her closer to the darkened yard where she was rebuilding her husband's palace. She stacked the future-wine-glasses and future-dining-chairs and future-children's-toys against the back wall of the cottage. From the front of the house, a voice.

'Sal? Is that you? Mate, I brought your mower back.'

Her husband! She felt her heart kick into double-time. Feet light, she skipped around to the front of the cottage.

There was her husband, lamplight-bathed, his face hidden as he peered into the living room window between his cupped hands. He jumped back as she twined her hand in his.

'Jesus Christ, Mirren! I nearly shat, you gave me such a fucking fright. Is he away?'

She pulled his hand behind her back, trapping herself between his body and the front door. She kissed the anchor tattooed on her husband's wrist.

'He's not here, is he? I was just saying that about the mower.'

She reached up and twisted her hair into a rope so that he could see the long pale line of her neck. Her husband loved her neck; she knew it made him think of swans, of Celtic goddesses, of carved ships' figureheads. She knew he loved and respected every part of her, but her delicate neck most of all.

'Oh, is that what you want? You always did like it rough, you dirty bitch.'

Her husband took the silken rope of her hair in his strong hands and wrapped it once, twice, three times around her throat. From the moment she'd seen that anchor, she knew that her husband was the one to keep her grounded. To stop her from floating away on the hungry sea towards her husband. To be her husband until she had her husband again. The anchor twitched as he pulled her hair tight around her throat.

'Mirren, alright! I've already let go! Don't shove me. I said don't fucking shove me. One more time and I'm gone.'

To her husband, she was everything: a goddess, a mother, an innocent. He worshipped her. She knew he did. He didn't have to say it. She wanted to show him that she was worshipping him too, in her own way.

'Are we fucking, or what? I haven't got long.'

She took her husband's hand and led him around to the back of the house. There, in the yard, lay the foundations of the palace. She was remaking it from the bones out. She wanted him to see her devotion.

'Mirren, fuck's sake. Stop messing about. I need to get home soon. She'll know that I'm not just dropping off the mower if I'm gone too long.'

She lay down in the centre of the palace, spreading her body out for her husband. This is how he would worship her: among the growing bones of the home she was rebuilding.

'You filthy bitch. You want me to fuck you there in the dirt? Outside, where anyone could see? Fucking filthy.'

Her husband smiled down at her and love glowed from his face. She reached for him, and he came to her. He was honest with love.

'I bet you're wet. Do you want my dick inside you?'

The anchor twisted fleshwise as he unfastened his trousers. She lifted herself up on her elbows, letting her hair cascade out of its rope and down her back. She leaned to kiss the anchor, to show her husband that she understood: that he was holding her here, grounding her in this good earth, because he cared. Because he loved her more than anything – even more than his sea-palace.

'Stop leaning up. I can't put it in when you're like that. Lie back down and lift up your skirt.'

She was loving her husband the way that he was loving her. He balanced over her on one arm, his hand flat on the ground, the anchor twitching. When her body connected with her husband's, she closed her eyes and saw the palace she was building for him.

'Ohhhh, yes. Keep still, Mirren.'

The polished brass grates. The intricately carved chairs. The filigree cutlery. The silken sheets. The painted china plates.

'Fuck. Ah yes, fuck.'

Her husband professed his love to her, in his body and in his movements, right then and there in the yard.

'Oh fuck. Stay still. I'm gonna fucking come.'

She kissed the anchor that kept her grounded. Her husband's skin smelled of woodsmoke.

September

Once a woman had her husband. Nothing mattered except that he was here. He'd left her for the sea but now he was home, and home was the whole world. He'd gone out tonight, but not far. Not to sea this time. Just a drink with the boys.

She tidied. She cooked. She pressed her hands to the walls, imagining him. How many walls between them? Two? Four? She could smash through them if she had to. Knowing she could meant that she didn't need to.

'I love you!' she called out. The words echoed through their house.

When she heard his key in the door, she thought perhaps she had summoned him. He'd heard her words through all those walls, and he had come to her.

She turned, ready to collapse into his arms. She stopped. He stood in the doorway, his face grey and still.

'I heard a story about you,' he said. 'It wasn't a good one.'

She moved towards him – to shut the door to the rest of the world, to make it the two of them again. No stories, or only good ones. But he put up his hands, palms towards her.

'Stop. Let me speak. The story – it was Douglas Unthank from the back farm. He was out in the field a couple of weeks ago. Teasing away, he was, asking if the wife had enjoyed her fun in the yard. Asking me if I'd enjoyed showing my arse to the sky. But I wasn't there, Mirren. I wasn't there. So who was there?'

Love swelled the back of her throat, pressed against the roof of her mouth. She could not speak. But it did not matter. Her silence held her confession. Her husband turned and walked away.

It was dawn before he came back. He shuffled down the hall and thudded into the bedroom door. The door opened in darkness and he dropped onto the bed, his limbs pressing awkwardly against hers. His breath came heavy as bellows. She reached for him, but he knocked her hand away. His next breath hitched into a sob.

'Why, Mirren?'

How could she explain that she loved him so much that she couldn't bear to be without him even for one night? That she loved him enough for two husbands? Her love filled her lungs, filled the full length of her legs. Her love overflowed her body.

'I love you,' she said.

'That's not a reason. Since I took this offshore job, I don't know what went wrong. All this junk in the yard – fucking another man – I don't even know you.'

'I –'

'You love me, I know, I know. But it's not just about you, Mirren. To be together, we can't always be together. You need something in your life other than me. I have to work. We have to live.'

She reached for him again. He rolled off the bed, thudding to his knees on the floor. He got up and stumbled out of the house, clicking the door shut behind him. She closed her eyes. Why didn't he understand? She loved him completely, blindly, consumingly, the way a woman should. There was no room inside her for anything except love. What else could she have in her life other than him?

She pressed her knuckles against her closed eyelids, watching the flashes of colour. She had nothing to cry about. Her husband was home.

October

Once there was a woman who had no husbands at all. She was completely empty, the love scooped out of her. She walked out of the house and down the path. She walked through the marram grass, feeling it scratch at her ankles. She walked across the spit and onto the sand. She walked into the water. Soon her feet left the seabed. She lifted her legs and turned her face to the sky. The water lapped at her temples and chin, filling her ears.

The moon hung, fat and bright. Floating here, she was not at sea, and she was not on land. She could not smell woodsmoke or saltwater.

She let herself sink down – but she realised that she was not sinking down, but up. The pull of the earth, the pull of the sea – they were both being pulled away from her. Or she was pushing them away from herself.

She opened her eyes and a summer sky spread wide for her. The cold moon had disappeared, replaced with a hot copper sun. She looked over her shoulder and already the sea was three body-lengths below her. She was lighter than a breeze. But she did not feel bloated to bursting, stuffed with love. She was beautifully empty. She did not need someone else to fill her up.

She breathed and her lungs filled like pink wings. Her bones felt hollow as a seabird's. Her heart was light and huge, the hugest thing she could imagine. It swelled and her chest seemed to expand, each rib spreading like the fingers of an unfurling fist. The wind blew through her and under her, lifting her higher.

Below her the earth shone green like a jewel. The sea glittered at her. The sun stroked her skin. She was warm and light, a feather on the breeze. She spread her arms and, empty, she soared.

Ruth:

Wave goodbye to your other mother, Coorie! No, no, don't
fidget now. She's going to work; she'll be home again soon.
Come on now, and we'll have some breakfast.

I think you'll like it here. I can't wait to show you how the morning sun slants through the kitchen window, the bright gold slats it makes across the table. They warm my hands here as I hold my teacup. But that won't be for long. I can never stay still. There's so much to do, so much to prepare for you. And I've barely begun telling you my stories.

Oh, how you fidget! Can't you give me a moment's peace? If you want your breakfast, you'll have to keep still and let me have mine. Even sitting on this chair is uncomfortable with your elbows and toes pushing at me. Sometimes I wish you out of me so I can be at rest.

I have work to do other than you, my Coorie. Yes, you are the sun of my world – but everyone has their own world, and you cast no light there. My work is to change other people's stories, but not so much that it's no longer their story. They call it ghost writing, and I always thought that meant that I was a ghost. Lately I've been thinking something else – perhaps in writing someone's story, I make them into a ghost. People in stories are not like living people – once they are written down, they can't change. It's better to tell the story of a person when they're gone, when they can't contradict what you decide they are. The dead are best for stories. The living make for terrible ghosts.

I must work now, because I know that when you come, there will be even less rest. I have to use this time well. There's so much I want to teach you. It would be better if I didn't have to sneak my stories into your ears. I know it seems strange that I wait for your other mother to leave, but you mustn't think that means we lie. We don't, not about anything else. But we agreed that we'd only ever tell you the truth – the plain truth, no frills or fripperies, and absolutely no stories. Our lives are all about stories, and we wanted something different for you. Lies can be a comfort, but a dangerous one.

This is a story about a story, told to me by a man you will meet someday. Me and your other mother are your parents, but we couldn't make you by ourselves. We needed help. So here is a story from the man who helped me to make you. You're half of him, and I'm telling you his story so that you understand that half – so that you can learn to overcome it, before it overcomes you.

5

The Animals Went in
Two by Two

Friday night at the Aberfeldy Fun Pit, and I'm centre-stage with all eyes on me. Well, not me exactly, but on Doggo the Dog, and inside him is me. It's hot under the fur suit, and I can't really see through the mesh screen of Doggo's mouth. But I'm a professional, so I don't miss a single step of the Weeble Wobble. Not like the kids. They're proper shit. Even later, at the Kidz Session, when I break the dance down into individual steps and show them slowly over and over, they still won't get it. So shit.

The lights are flashing red-blue-green, and all the kids and the parents are clapping out of time. But Leila and Frankie and Roz don't miss a beat. They're up on their feet, clapping and singing – they know all the words now too, this is the third day of their holiday and they've come along every night. Some folk get bored of it, stay in their caravans, bring bottles of wine from home and drink out on their little plastic porches instead, get wrapped up in coats and scarves when it gets chilly, the bright ends of their fags making constellations as you walk through the park. But not Leila and Frankie and Roz. Not as long as I'm Doggo the Dog.

It's embarrassing that they're seeing me like this. What I mean is that I'm embarrassed. They're not embarrassed, not at all, not ever and especially not now. They're gleeful. They're loving this. They're not even embarrassed on my behalf, which I suppose is good, because if this was an actual genuine shame-fest then they'd all be shuffling their feet and looking away, not clapping and cheering me on. Like a few years ago, I knew I'd put on too much weight when they stopped calling me Fat Boy or Pie Muncher. If something is a tiny bit out of the ordinary, folk can make a joke of it. But if something is really a problem, like a serious embarrassing problem, then no one talks about it. So I got my fat arse to the gym, ate chicken and broccoli for every dinner, and got right into shape. Then when I was buff as fuck, they started calling me Fat Boy again, and I knew I was fine.

I'm nearly at the end of the Weeble Wobble now, almost at the bit where I have to turn around and wiggle my rear end. I bet all the mums and dads wouldn't find it so funny if they knew it was a camp wee gay-boy inside the suit; that I'd wiggled my arse plenty times before this, and even for one or two of the dads staying at the park.

After that I do my bow – the wrong way, facing the stage, so that the kids can have a wee laugh at Doggo's rear end again. Kids never get tired of arse jokes. Then we have a break, but I can't take my head off in case the kids see, so when Leila and Frankie and Roz tumble over to me I have to talk to them through the mesh screen of the dog's mouth.

'Bravo!' roars Frankie. 'Bra-fucking-vo! Your best performance yet, Doggo. The Academy will be in touch.'

'Aye, fuck off, Frankie,' I say, chucking him under his stubbled chin with my paw. 'I'd like to see you try.'

'Get your kit off and I will.' He makes to tug off Doggo's head. I put my paws over his hands to stop him. He can't see whether I'm smiling, but his grin assumes I am. I'm not. We're messing, I know, but he couldn't do this. It's not as easy as it looks.

'Same again?' says Leila, nodding to the bar. 'Anything for you, Doggo? Bowl of water? Bone biscuit?'

'Nah, thanks.' I've got a bottle of water in the staff room, but I don't want to tell Leila that I can't have anything because I can't take my head off. Leila sashays to the bar, wiggling her arse for the dads, and Frankie slopes off to the loo. Roz stays behind, and my vision is so crap through the mesh screen that I hadn't noticed she's been resting her hand on my fur-thick forearm.

'You're doing good,' she says.

'Superman does good,' I say, and I grin all toothy even though she can't see it. 'I'm doing *well*.'

Roz smiles prettily, eyes limpid and lips shiny, and pats my – Doggo's – arm before going back to her table. She knows I'm gay, like, but she's still giving it a go. Good on her – it might even work. Everyone's curious, aren't they? Then the lights are back on, the music's up, and it's time for the Kidz Session to begin and for the adults to get down to proper drinking. First I show them the Weeble Wobble, which is most definitely not the Hokey Cokey because although we do say *you put your right hand in, you put your right hand out*, there's no shaking it about – we weeble wobble it about. Not the same at all.

Then I time which kid can say 'laaaaaa' the longest. It's hard not to flinch back when some of these kids open their gappy, chocolatey gobs and shout 'LAAAAA' right in my face, but I'm a great actor so I manage it no bother. I'll tell you something, though: I've never been more grateful for that mesh screen. Then it's time for the individual talents. I'm being generous here in my use of the word 'talent'. Mostly it's kids singing that song from *Frozen*, their voices whispery and flat, or doing a clumsy dance to some Taylor Swift pop racket. At least there aren't any amateur magicians tonight; they're the worst. The kid's shaking hands, the flimsy plastic tricks, everyone pretending they can't see the way the corners of the false cards are folded.

It wasn't always like this. When I was a kid, my folks took me here, and there were talent scouts in the audience. Like, real talent scouts, looking for real talent. I didn't know about them the first night because my parents didn't tell me – or maybe they didn't know, but at the time I didn't think of that because when you're a kid you think all adults know everything, don't you? Until you become a teenager and realise that no adults know anything at all.

Anyway, after the first night my Uncle Eli joined us, and he told me about the talent scouts. When I did my talent – a different one every night it was, singing and dancing and reciting, and not a sodding magic trick to be seen – the scouts were just blown away. I was head and shoulders above the other kids. I didn't win every night, obviously, because that wouldn't have been fair. It wasn't a real talent show; it was just to keep the parents and kids happy. The talent scouts could see the difference in me, but they couldn't come forward at the time because, like Uncle Eli said, officially they were there on their holidays and not scouting talent, so it would have been unprofessional for them to approach me. Even then it was obvious that I was different. Better. A natural talent.

I pick the fattest kid to win the individual talents. I feel sorry for him, and anyway he does have a good singing voice. Bigger lungs, maybe, to get the oxygen to all his fatty limbs. I present him with his prize – a cuddly toy with scary eyes, a colouring book he's too old for, and drinks tokens for his already-drunk parents – bow to the kids, waggle my rear end once more, and then, fucking finally, I can leave. In the staff room I peel off my sweaty fur and drink the whole bottle of water in one go. Quick spray under the arms, change of t-shirt, and Doggo is done for the night.

I slip in beside Roz just as the quiz is starting. She looks me up and down, eyelashes flicking.

'Queeeestion one!' says the quizmaster into the mic, his mouth far too close so we can all hear his wet breath. It's something about the Falklands, and I know fuck all about that, and I think about making a joke, like *I know falk all about the Falklands*, but honestly I can't be bothered. Doggo really sucks out my soul sometimes.

I gulp at the pint that Frankie's put in front of me and peer round at the other tables. If the parents know that I'm Doggo, they're keeping it hush-hush. The next table over is piled with shimmer lip-gloss, wrinkled Capri-Sun cartons, and a wine bottle dripping onto a paper hat. The fish and chips are served in a child's plastic bucket, with a spade on the side. If it's early in the season and the waitresses aren't too bored yet, they kid on that folk have to use that unwieldy plastic spade to eat their chips. Shovel them up, like. And to be honest, going by the size of some of these families – girth-wise as well as the actual quantity of them – I'd believe that they do eat chips with a shovel.

'Oy! Doggo!' Frankie's starting to slur his words now, but it snaps me awake. 'Was it hot at the millennium? We were, like, four years old then. Can you remember being four?'

'It was December,' adds Leila, 'so it can't have been hot.'

'Fuck sake, Lei, that's the point of the question! It was a heat*wave*, like unusual heat, not normal-time heat. Look, I don't remember it being cold. Do you remember that? I don't remember that. I was barely born, for fuck's sake. I'm writing true. There was a heatwave. It's true.'

'Nah,' I say, my memories coming together slowly, treacle-wading. 'Nah, that's wrong, cos I mind the weather at the millennium. It was cold. Really cold, like a snowstorm.'

'Oh aye?' says Leila. 'You're the Rain Man, are you? Got a catalogue of past weather events logged in your head?'

'Shut up. I just remember that one. It was a party, and there was snow, and my uncle brought animals. Loads of them, real ones, tigers and elephants and that.'

Leila snorts. 'Eh – what?'

'You mean balloon animals? Cardboard cut-outs?' Frankie can hardly get the words out past his sloppy sniggers. 'Wee stuffed toys? Mate, sorry to break it, but they ain't real.'

'No, look, I remember. Write false, Frankie. There wasn't a heatwave, there was snow. Loads of it, a snowstorm. I'm sure. I remember, that was why the animals couldn't come inside, because the snow was –'

Frankie's shushing me, and I can see he's written *false* so really I should give it up, but I want to keep talking because it's a cool story.

I want to remind them that I am cool, despite the song and the wiggling rear end and everything.

Frankie and Leila are listening to the next question – or rather, queeeestion – but Roz is still looking at me. She opens her mouth to ask me, but I make a big show of frowning like I'm listening to the quiz. It's not that I don't want to tell Roz. It's just that I want to tell Leila and Frankie too. I was a cool and unusual kid that cool and unusual things happened to, and I'm still cool now, and the fact that I dress up in a Doggo the Dog costume just makes me cooler. Like when George Clooney dressed up like a chicken when he was young – or maybe that was Brad Pitt. Ethan Hawke, maybe? Anyway, their coolness now is enhanced by the lameness of that, because it shows that even though they did that shit, they were above it. They did it, but they didn't do it the way a mere mortal would have done it. Even dressed as a chicken, I bet Brad Pitt was cool.

At the millennium we were having a party, or I mean my mum and dad were having a party. I was six, or almost six, because my birthday is on the first of January but no one wants to have a party then so I always had it on Hogmanay. There was sugar-gritty cake, and paper plates, and someone's gummy wee brother rubbed his one tooth on a balloon until it popped.

At tea-time my mum started handing out party bags, and everyone made as if to leave, so I had to go round taking back the party bags and tipping them out on the floor. No one could leave because Uncle Eli wasn't there yet. It was my party and I'd say when everyone could leave.

But it didn't matter, not even when I hid up in my room with my back against the door, because I could hear that the house was getting quieter and quieter as everyone left. Then it was dark and I felt sick from all the cake and the snow came on, and at first it was magical, so magical that I stopped crying, the fact that it was snowing just for me, but then it came on stronger and I could hardly see, and when I opened the window to try to catch a snow-flake loads of it blew in hard and covered me and the carpet, and my mum shouted. Later I was bath-warm and tucked up in my pyjamas when the doorbell rang. I stood on my bed to look out of the window, but I couldn't see who it was through the snow. A few minutes later Uncle Eli bundled into my room, smelling of cold and cigarette smoke, and dropped a present at the foot of my bed, like Santa. He went *sssshhhh*! with his forefinger pressed to his lips, then crept out again.

I'd only just thrown back my duvet to open the present when the doorbell rang again. I sat motionless, listening. The door opening. Uncle Eli talking. The door closing. Thump-thump-thump up the stairs.

'That was the giraffe! She came for your party but she's late because she got lost in the snow. She wanted to pop her head in your window, but your mum said you were sleeping. She brought you a present.' And he popped another wrapped box at the foot of my bed. When he left, I reached for the present – but the doorbell rang again! Door opening, door closing, thump-thump-thump.

'That was the lion!' Uncle Eli was panting now, from all the run-ning up and down the stairs. 'It's a bit chilly for him so he had to keep moving. It's awful snowy out there, you should have seen that poor lion shaking it off his mane.' And he dropped another box at the foot of my bed.

After that the elephant, the tiger and the seal all stopped by, all with gifts, but all too chilly to stay. I always knew I was special, and here was the proof: the only boy in the whole town who got real live animals at their party. When I opened the presents it turned out they weren't really separate presents, they were all the parts of a train set – a train in one box, a carriage in another, some tracks in another – and they all added up to one big present. The animals were so clever to plan it like that. I climbed up on my bed and looked out of the window, my feet crackling among the torn wrapping paper. I was sure, through the blowing snow, that I saw the animals walking away.

Everyone else gets the snowstorm question wrong and we win the quiz. The prize is a crate of beer; Frankie carries it back to the caravan on his shoulders, singing *Hi-ho, hi-ho*.

That night, after we've drunk all the beers and Frankie and Leila have disappeared into the bedroom and Roz has passed out on the couch and I'm back in my own caravan, I bring up Google on my phone. I can't stop thinking about the animals coming to my birthday party. I haven't thought about it in years, but now it's all coming back so strong. I suppose the memory was sitting in my brain all that time, getting stronger, getting more entrenched. I keep my eyes mainly on the TV, though, because I'm not really Googling anything. Who Googles their own memories? That would be stupid. I'm not doubting myself and I'm not doubting Uncle Eli. I'm just looking.

And yes, okay, so now that I think about it Uncle Eli always turned up late, always a day or two into the trip, and always at night.

Like Santa, and I remember picturing Uncle Eli's glamorous life, existing entirely after dark, all women and fast cars like James Bond. Santa mixed with James Bond – what the fuck was I thinking? Kids are weird.

And yes, he had red cheeks and a red nose and his breath always smelled like booze, but adults drink, don't they? I remember all adults being drunk. Not all the time, and not like messy drunk, not angry or violent or horrible, just the usual. Tipsy, silly. Your dad bragging about past sporting events and trying to do one-arm push-ups. Your mum creeping into your room to plant a sloppy kiss on your cheek, breathing G&Ts all over you. Uncle Eli staggering around crowing that he was someone, he was special, he was someone. Uncle Eli passed out on the couch, snoring like a giant as I ate my cornflakes. Uncle Eli, waking at lunchtime and skulking away, his bloodshot eyes refusing to meet my mum's. Everyone did that. I mean, if Uncle Eli was an alcoholic then Leila and Frankie and Roz are fucking pathological.

I glance down at my phone, look back at the TV. It's a talent show. Maybe I'll phone in and vote for the shittest one, just for a laugh. Then I notice it's two a.m. and realise it's a repeat. Did anyone else tell me about the talent scouts apart from Uncle Eli? Did he ever say it in front of the other adults? He did. I'm sure he did. It was a fact. No one's talked about it for a while, but I'm sure we talked about it a lot at the time. I remember.

I scroll and scroll through the Google results. Nothing, nothing, and I'm about to give up and play a game instead – then, on some weird true news stories site, I see it.

MERRY CHIMP-MAS!
Residents stunned as wild animals roam free

The article says that a local farmer was breeding illegal animals – monkeys, lions, even seals – but got a tip-off that the police were going to raid his farm. He released all the animals into the countryside so that he couldn't get done for having them. They roamed around all night before the SSPCA or the zoo or whoever could get the proper folk and equipment to round them all up. And who's to say, really, that those animals couldn't have wandered past my house? Who's to say they couldn't have come to my door? So there it is. There's the proof. I don't even need to show Leila and Frankie and Roz because it's enough that I know.

I should sleep, but I don't want to go into the tiny bedroom; I'm too tall for the bed and the sheets are always a bit damp. I lie on the couch, cover myself with my coat, and let the sound of the TV lull me. As I drift off, I think that it doesn't even matter if Uncle Eli did lie. It doesn't matter about the animals or the talent scouts. Because whatever else is true about that night, it's true that Uncle Eli brought presents, just for me. I am special. I've always been special. And soon, I'll be someone.

Liska:

Listen. You're getting big now, almost big enough for the world. And I can see that you're restless, never letting your mama sit at peace. But now, I want you to let her sleep, and listen to me. Push past the sounds of your mama's body: her slow-thudding heart, the swoop of her lungs. Do you hear how the night gulls wheel above us? Do you hear them shrieking their lullabies? It's rancid and raucous, I know, but that is simply their voice. And we can only ever speak in the voice we're given. For a long time after I left Norway, I felt that my voice wasn't right. It marked me out as different, when all I wanted was to fit in. I said nothing at all for such a long time. Then one day I met your mama, and I realised I had something to say – and more importantly, someone I wanted to say it to. Now I talk for a living, but I save all my best words for her.

Everything in the world speaks, and right now our home is speaking to you. The walls creak their approval in the wind. The rain applauds on the roof. The lighthouse beam swoops, swoops, swoops. The tide breathes loud and slow as a giant. If you listen carefully, perhaps you can even hear the moon hum.

That's good, that's right, you settle down. It's not that I don't like to see your tiny fists, your tiny feet, trying to fight their way into the world. I love to imagine you. But you must let your mama rest. When I picture you, I can't decide: are you a boy or are you a girl? We don't know, my little seahorse, and so you can be either, and so you can be both. However you grow, you must learn to speak in your own true voice. And I have a story about that very thing, told to me by a good friend. Perhaps you will meet him someday; perhaps, if you ask nicely, he will take us all out on his fishing boat.

Climb in, my tiny fish-catcher, and I will take you on a journey.

6

Flinch

I always get up early so I can be out early. Of all the fishermen in Sanctuary, I'm out the earliest. I have to be. It explains why I bring the most back.

In the summer half-light I steer my electric bike along the winding cliffside roads. Its mechanical burr throbs through my bones. Two miles away from the house I pull the bike up onto the grassy edge of a passing place. No need to lock it. If anyone from Sanctuary stole it, they'd have to hide it in their shed forever or I'd see it and steal it right back. There's no use in taking something you can't use.

I unpack my waterproofs from the bike's seat storage and pull them on over my cotton jogging suit. I heft three crates from the back of the bike, down over the slippery rocks, and into the little motorboat. Rain sloshes in the bottom. I scoop some out with half a plastic jug before giving up. It doesn't matter. With a rrr-rrr-hhhrrr the motorboat's engine grumbles awake. I steer it out towards the fishing boat.

The sky is pinkish-grey like the insides of shells. Speckled bonxies wheel overhead. Seals loll on the rocks, fat as kings. The rising mist is cool and milky. I anchor the motorboat and transfer the crates onto the fishing boat, one foot on each deck. I heft with the rhythm of my breaths. The air is cold in my lungs.

I drop the crates into the vivier tank, making sure that the tubes are connected to bring in a constant stream of seawater. The langoustines I catch will stay alive until the moment they're dropped into the pot of boiling water. I start the engine and steer out to sea. Waves sway the boat, tilting the horizon. I slacken my knees to stay upright. It's easier beneath the water – it's quiet down there, and the waves soothe and rock like lullabies. On the surface, it's a constant battle to keep balance.

I keep sailing, out towards the sun. I want langoustine. They live in mud burrows, but the land near the shore is too hard for them. To get a good catch, a fisherman has to be willing to lose sight of the shore.

I reach down for the bait tub and heft it up onto the boat's side. Its seawater stink lingers in the lee behind the wheelhouse, and I exhale hard to push the smell out of my throat. I slice the fish into three. A palm-size piece to bait the creels. Gulls perch along the back of the boat, cawing for morsels.

I reach the buoy that marks the start of my first fleet. I keep five fleets, with fifty creels per fleet. The other Sanctuary fishermen have more: Douglas Unthank has fifteen fleets, Alasdair Macleod has twenty, John and Samson Burr have forty between them. But for me, five fleets is just enough to look reasonable. Folk might wonder why my creels always haul in the most, but it's still believable.

I take the boat out of gear, and to the sounds of its low grumble I start to reel in the first fleet. The creels thud up the side of the boat in a steady rhythm, one every thirty seconds. I haul the creel, open it, empty it, rebait it, stack it. Steady as heartbeats, as the slap of waves on the dock, as steps along a road.

The langoustine I pull from the creels go into the vivier tank, sorted by size. Medium, large, or good money. The smallest ones are thrown in a bucket. Crabs and dogfish get thrown back into the water. A man has to be very hungry before he'll eat a dogfish. Any torn creels get thrown to the side, for me to reattach after I've repaired them. About a third of creels come up empty; I pull out the uneaten bait and toss it to the gulls. If I see the black blobs of eggs crusted along the langoustines' undersides, they go back into the sea. No use in catching the pregnant ones now when I could wait and take their grown-up babies. Don't take more than you need.

When the emptied, re-baited creels are hauled in and stacked three-high in the back of the boat, I put the engine back in gear. I kick the first creel into the water and go back into the wheelhouse. The weight of that first creel will pull the others back into the sea one by one. The most useful thing I can do is keep my feet well away from the twisting ropes. Everyone knows about the time Donald Unthank got his ankle caught and ended up in the freezing January water, with a hefty thud to his head as he went in. Good luck for Donald that his brother Douglas was there, and could haul his shivering body back onto the boat. Most of the fishermen go out in pairs. But I can't.

The final creels thunder between the boat's high sides on their way back to the water. I turn the boat and head for the next fleet. I lift the bucket of the smallest langoustine. The gulls and bonxies rise in a cloud from their perch on the back of the boat, shrieking and wheeling, swooping close to the water's mirrored surface. I top and tail the langoustine, their pinkish shells crunching between my hands. I throw their beady-eyed heads and insect-twitching legs to the birds. Their meaty bodies go into a clean container.

Five times I do the routine. Haul the creel, open, empty, rebait, stack, reshoot. One fleet per hour, two hundred and fifty creels in total. My buckets and vivier tanks are still half-empty. That's fine. They'll be full by the time I head home.

I stop the boat at the furthest-away point, far from the orange buoys that mark the other fishermen's fleets. Everyone has their patch. I know the other boats, and the other boats know me. They won't come close enough to see whether I'm in the wheelhouse, and anyway I've let the side windows grow opaque with rain and grime. It's time to start the real fishing.

I reach down and take off my boots and my thick woollen socks. I take off my waterproof trousers and my cotton jogging bottoms. I take off my waterproof jacket and my cotton sweatshirt. My bare skin tenses and prickles in the cool air. My toes stretch to grip the deck.

I tuck my discarded clothes into a kit bag in the wheelhouse. I gather up my net. I climb onto the ledge at the back of the boat. I dive in.

That evening, at the Inn, Tom Flinch is holding court. His wee mum, Mairi Flinch, rules the bar, pixie-small as she is, her fluffed gold hair and slippery pink smile, her little tanned hands pulling pints and skooshing out Coke fast as you like. But everything on the public side of the bar belongs to Tom Flinch.

'Right, boyo!' he caws when I walk in. 'Got a good catch for us the night?' He well knows my name – he's known it since school, the two of us always assigned neighbouring seats, linked by the alphabet – but he never seems to use it. I don't know why.

'Aye, Tom. The creels brought up the biggest langoustine I've seen in a year. Lots of eating in it. Enough for two.'

'Ah, you're the man. You staying on for your dinner?'

'Can't, Tom.'

'Ah, go on. We've got a nice list tonight. Mackerel cooked in butter with a dab of sea salt. Lovely bit of steak? Or there's king scallops. Comes with garlic butter, and bacon crisped up nice, and rice and salad and a wee bit bread too. Keep you full for days, that will.'

'No. Thanks though. Got to get home.'

'Fair enough. Bring it on through.' He swings his arm wide, like a stage magician, to lead my way to the kitchen. I make sure not to brush against him as I pass.

I heft the crates of langoustine into the walk-in refrigerator. The muscles in my shoulder pull and tense, and I concentrate on that, on the burning ache, never once looking behind me to see if Tom followed me into the kitchen. By the time the full crates are stacked and I've found yesterday's now-empty crates, goosebumps are pulling tight on my forearms. I turn. Tom is not there.

The kitchen is an organised chaos of gleaming counters and flames licking up around copper pans, smells of butter and fresh herbs, sizzles and slaps and slicing. There is a chef and a kitchen porter and two waiters all bobbing and weaving round one another, armed with white plates. But no Tom.

I heft the empty crates back out into the Inn. Tom fidgets at the head of a big table, each seat of which is occupied by one of the men from the salmon farm. One of them is holding up a langoustine from his plate, pretending to stab it in the head with a steak fork. The boys are all laughing. Tom fidgets more.

'You want a shot, Tom?' the man wielding the langoustine asks. 'Hone your stone-cold killer skills?'

'Meet Tom Flinch,' intones another man in a kid-on American voice, as if he's in a film trailer. 'Destroyer of seals. Saver of salmon. Stealer of hearts.'

I don't need to say anything to Tom so I won't; I'll just go straight out of the door and strap the crates onto my bike and go home. Head down, I barrel through the bar and out the front door. Safe.

I strap on the crates and reach for my helmet – then realise I'm one crate short. I consider leaving it, picking it up tomorrow when I drop off the catch. But then I'll have one fewer crate I can fill. We can't afford that. One less crate means one less meal on our table, one less mortgage payment, one less instalment on the gas bill. Head down, back through the Inn, without listening, without looking, into the kitchen, into the walk-in refrigerator, grab the missing crate, turn to leave.

The kitchen's back door is ajar, letting in a sliver of darkness. The cold breeze raises goosebumps on my arms again. Crate in hand, I lean outside. At the back door, Tom Flinch is lighting a cigarette. He flicks the flame alive with his thumb and cups his other hand against the wind. He closes his eyes and inhales deeply, as if he's trying to pull the smoke down into his thighs.

'You all right, Tom?'

'Aye.'

Silence. He doesn't open his eyes. I put the crate upside-down on the ground and sit on it. I cross my arms against the chill.

'You killed a seal today?' I say.

'Aye.'

'I wish you wouldn't.'

'Ah, come on. I had to.'

'There are ways around these things. You know there are.'

'And *you* know it's not that easy. The seals tear holes in the fences and snatch the salmon, and then the fish farm loses money. You know I don't like it, but I had to.'

'Still. I wish you wouldn't.'

'Aye, well. Me too.'

As Tom inhales, the tip of his cigarette glows bright. He exhales, and a haze of smoke rises up to the pinpricked sky. He won't know it does that, because his eyes are still closed. He won't know that I'm watching him smoke. He won't know that I'm looking up at him, and that his face is obscuring the stars.

I don't know what to say, so I don't say anything. I slide off the crate and bend to pick it up. As I straighten, I breathe in silent and deep, pulling the smoke inside me.

My mother was a slut. That's what the folk in Sanctuary said, and it's what they'll keep saying, even though she had me at eighteen and hasn't been with a man since. Some stains fade with time, but not this one.

She's waiting when I get in, with dinner on the table. Steam still hovering over the plates. She always knows exactly when I'll be back, even when I don't know myself.

'Good day today?' she says by way of greeting, bobbing up to dab a kiss on my cheek.

'Good enough,' I reply. I line my boots up by the door, wash my hands at the kitchen sink. 'That smells good.'

'It's only a bit mince and tatties, and you know it! Now sit yourself down.'

My mother fell in love all of a sudden, she said, with a man she just met. She worked at the Inn in those days, the gleaming-haired barmaid that made all the lads wink but wouldn't have a one of them. Perhaps they were all angry about that. Perhaps that's why they delighted so much in spreading the rumours later.

After she'd closed up the Inn one night, she walked away down the road to her house, and bumped right into a man. Literally bumped, so she spilled her handbag and scraped her knee on the ground. He lifted her clear in his arms, and the full moon lit up his face, and my mother was lost. His lips tasted of salt. She loved him, and in that moment he loved her too. Afterwards, in the misty dawn, she watched him walk across the shore and disappear into the sea. No one else ever saw a single hair on his head or heard a single scuff of his feet. Later, when my mother started to fatten with me, the folk in Sanctuary said he must have been a traveller, a gypsy boy just passing through, chancing his luck with the local girls.

No, my mother said. No, he wasn't that. But how could she explain what he was? She couldn't, so she didn't.

'How was the Inn looking?' she asks, after carefully chewing and swallowing a forkful of buttery potato.

'Grand,' I reply. 'Well, fine. Busy.'

'How's Mairi Flinch coping with the bar?'

I choose my words. 'Looked a bit harassed, to be honest. Lots of tables needed clearing.'

My mother glows. 'Well. That'll come with experience. She hasn't got the knack. But she'll learn.'

'You'd think she'd have learned by now. Years and years she's been there.'

'Hush, you! I won't hear a bad word in this house. If you can't say anything nice, don't say anything at all.'

'Yes, Mum.' Out of the corner of my eye, I see her secret grin. Ever since I was born, she's had to travel fifty miles up the road to work at the restaurant in the hotel. It's not so bad, but I know she misses the Inn. There's too much pride and old whispering now for her to ever go back there.

The Sanctuary folk, they don't understand love like my mum knew it. They cast their nets casually, never looking at what they might catch, eating whatever they drag up. But I know something of that man, something even my mother doesn't.

'Out early again tomorrow?' she asks.

'Aye. Don't you be getting up, though. I'll get my breakfast.'

'I'll leave you something out. Bread and cheese, maybe?' She's finished eating, and she leaves her plate and goes over to the sink. She runs hot water over the dinner pans. 'Cereal's not enough,' she says, 'Not when you're out on the boat all day.'

'Anything's fine, Mum.'

'You're a good lad. Best fisherman in the town, no doubt about that. You make your mum proud.' She busies herself at the sink. She keeps murmuring, but she's not really listening to herself. 'Don't know where you get it from, so I don't. I could never get my sea legs! The water is fine enough from the shore, thank you very much.'

My mother was beautiful once, in the way that milkmaids in old paintings are beautiful. I've seen photos: she had high cheekbones, eyes as blue as summer skies, lips red like cherries in the snow. But children can scratch away at the deepest beauty. The years of bending to lift me have stooped her back; the thousands of times she had wiped my dirty hands and my dirty face have reddened her pale hands.

I am the proof, the truth about the man she loved. I get a reliable haul, no matter the weather. Even in a storm, I fill my langoustine baskets. I can catch a fish in silty water. I never need to fear drowning. But I'm not brave like my mother. She was never afraid of the whispers, the judgements. She always held her head high. She refused to move away from Sanctuary, even when they told her not to come back to the Inn. She didn't bother about not having a man. She kept the fires burning and dinner on the table, no matter how much the gossips longed to see her fail. She can tell the truth. I can't.

I have a good life. I make enough. I feed myself and my mother, and I keep a roof over our heads. I'm careful with my hauls, never taking too much, preserving fish stocks for future generations. I have time off to live a life, to catch my breath.

'That was lovely,' I say, pushing away my plate. 'I couldn't eat another bite.'

'Good lad. Look, there's a wee bitty of mine left too. I'll pack up both our leftovers for your lunch tomorrow.'

'Aye,' I say. 'Thanks, Mum.'

The TV swallows the rest of the evening. I doze off on the couch, jolt awake to the sound of the ten o'clock news, drag myself up to my bed.

I wake at the bottom of the sea. Above me on the surface, my pillows float like lily pads. When I look properly, I see that the seafloor isn't sand, but my mattress. I try to kick off, to reach the surface, but my foot is tangled. I look down and I'm caught in a creel, the woven rope scraping at my ankle. I push out all my breath so that I sink small, small, small enough to slip in between the holes in the ropes, to hunker down at the bottom of the creel, to cover my eyes with mud. I hide there until I fall asleep, until I wake.

I get up early so I can be out early. Summer half-light and my electric bike's mechanical burr in my bones. Cotton jogging suit, waterproofs. I haul creels, open them, empty them, rebait them, stack them, reshoot them from the deck. Then into the water for the real catch.

When night starts creeping in, I take my crates of langoustine over to the Inn. It's a clear night, the air cold and the stars bright. Through the wide window I see Mairi Flinch handing Tom two trays of drinks, which he balances effortlessly as he strides between the chattering tables. It'll be a busy night. They'll need everything I caught. I heft my crates through the door.

'Ah, the haul's here!' Trays now empty, Tom approaches me. He hasn't combed his hair properly; a tuft fans out at the crown.

'Aye, Tom,' I say. 'Plenty langoustine tonight.'

'You're a good man. Go on and stay for dinner. We've got trout. I saved you a nice fat piece. It's rolled in oatmeal and baked among the coals, so outside it's crunchy but the inside will flake apart on your tongue.'

My shoulders ache; the crates' edges dig into my legs. 'On my what?'

He smiles. 'Your tongue.'

And I can almost taste it then, the baked crunch of the pinhead oatmeal, the sweetness of that fresh pink fish as it crumbles to flakes in my mouth.

'Can't, Tom. Got to –'

'Got to get home. Aye, I know. Well, on you go into the kitchen. You know the way.'

I stack the refrigerator shelves with the day's catch and retrieve yesterday's empty crates. The kitchen door swings open to admit a waiter. Through the gap I get a glimpse of Tom, announcing the daily specials to a table of red-lipped women.

On my way back out with the empty crates, I flinch at a shriek. It slips into laughter. The table of women are giggling fit to burst.

'On my tongue! Did you hear him?'

'Fancy you, talking about a lady's tongue.'

'You've a cheek, you wee charmer.'

I think of their shiny lips closing around a lump of trout as Tom looks on. Back to my bike, helmet on. Above me, the stars wink. The sea wind brings the slightest touch of smoke. I've forgotten a crate.

The kitchen is empty, except for the chefs and kitchen porters and waiters. I lift the forgotten crate and go back through the Inn. Shouts from the table, the men from the salmon farm.

'Cheer up, Flinchy. It might never happen.'

'Get the round in, that'll cheer you up.'

'Ah, you big gayboy! You're not still weeping over that dead seal?'

I don't mean to look over at Tom Flinch. I really don't. All I want to do is get on my bike and ride off down the road until the noise of the Inn is overtaken by the sea's shushing. But that word – it catches me in the chest, snags me like a fishhook.

I look over at him, and he is looking back at me. The fishhook twists. As I walk away I feel it tug at the skin over my heart and pull, pull, pull.

That night my mother is working late at the hotel. I'd forgotten, and I arrive home to a darkened house and a note taped to the fridge. Some clan convention thing: Americans touring around Scotland in their mouldy old tartans, going out on boat trips and shooting at deer. I imagine she'll amp up the 'ochs' in her talk, patter around like a bonny wee lassie. She'll keep her smile wide and she'll never stop moving long enough for them to spy the wrinkles. In candlelight she's a bonny lassie still, despite me. She'll get good tips.

I ding a meal in the microwave and eat it standing over the sink. I rinse my fork, put the packet in the bin, and that's the washing-up done. The evening stretches. Every time I blink I see red lips closing over pink lumps of trout. I open up all the cupboards, not really knowing what I'm looking for, until I see the thing and realise. Whisky: the colour of autumn leaves and smelling of peat. The bottle that Mum says she saves for Hogmanay, but steals a wee nip at when she's had a bad day at the hotel. She generally has good days, so the bottle is almost full. The light catches it. It glows.

I put on some music and tip crisps in a bowl. I pour whisky into one of the fancy glasses and sit at the kitchen table. I'm not a sad man drinking alone – it's a party! There's music and food! The glass keeps emptying so I keep refilling it. The music ends and I don't restart it. I push the crisps away. I drink and drink and when the bottle is empty I wish it full again – not of drink, but of a ship. A miniature ship, with matchstick masts and a plywood deck, a gathering of sails each as small as a tooth. A person could go far with such a ship, if where they wanted to go was already close by.

Red lips. Red lips and pink trout, melting sweetly on the tongue. And why can't I stay for dinner, just once? Why can't he know? Is it so strange? Is there a harm in it, really? Maybe he'd understand. Maybe he'd even be glad. I have a good life. It's enough. It should be enough.

I rinse out my glass and switch off all the lights before I leave. My mother taught me well: an empty heart is not an excuse to go out without a coat on. To let pans boil over or the fire die down. To forget to hold doors open or say please or pass the potatoes round before taking some for yourself.

The Inn is loud as a storm. Lights blaze against the night. Dinner is over, the kitchen is closed. Only the proper drinkers remain. The men from the salmon farm seem to have expanded, taking up half the room.

'That table's gone,' I say. Tom Flinch stops collecting glasses onto a tray and looks at me. I'm sure he glances around to see who's watching before he replies.

'What table?'

'The one. Wanting the fishes and the tongue. The one with the women.' The words aren't coming out right, but it must be right enough because he laughs.

'Ah, women. They're tricksy things. They think everything that comes out of their mouths is roses and everything that comes out of yours is dirt.'

84

I focus on his face, trying not to scrunch up my eyes. 'You don't like them? You seemed to like them. Women. You like women. The table, I mean.'

'I like some of them, and I don't like some of them, same as with men.'

I want to tell him that I understand. Women are a foreign country. Nice enough, but that I've no interest in visiting. I don't say that. Instead I say: 'Come out with me. On the boat. Tomorrow.'

Tom looks over at the table of his friends, laughing and raising their glasses. Loud and proud as Vikings.

'In the morning? Och, I don't know, man. Not really a morning person. And I'll be working late tonight, shutting up the bar and that, so I won't be up until –'

'Tom.' I'm not sure he hears me. The silence lasts forever. At least, it would be silence if we weren't in the noisiest building in Sanctuary. Blood throbs in my ears.

'Aye,' he finally says. 'Aye, you're right. A bit of sea air will do a body good. And it'll be useful for me to understand better how you get the catch. For the customers, like. And maybe there'll be some seals out. I'd like to see them and not have to shoot at them.'

'I'll pick you up,' I say. 'Tomorrow, at five.'

An expression scrunches Tom's face. He's about to protest – I can already hear his voice in my head: *Five a.m! That's practically the night before! No human should be up before the birds!* But his brow smoothes out and he nods.

'Okay,' he says. 'Okay, James. I'll be there.'

He'll be there. I feel sick. I nod at him and stride in what I think is a steady way out of the Inn. I want to raise my shoulders in defence, to hunch away from the laughs of the men from the salmon farm. But that would only draw attention. They're just laughing. They don't know anything.

The road is dark, lit by the moon's reflection on the water. My breathing is loud in my ears. I make it halfway down the road before I stumble into the grass, and everything I drank down comes back up. I cough and spit and crawl away from the mess of myself. The grass is cool and soft. I lie on my back and let the stars soothe me. I'll go home soon. It's not far. I'll go soon. And tomorrow – tomorrow I will –

The next morning, hungover and tender. I ride my bike limpingly along the road to the Inn. The day is too bright and too quick. Everything is moving at double speed, caught in a fast wind, tilting too close to the waves. I hold on tight to keep from capsizing. And then I see Tom Flinch outside the Inn, hunched bleary-eyed over a steaming mug. I stop the bike and put both feet flat on the ground.

'Morning,' he says, and the way he says it, the way he smiles, his mouth, I don't think I can –

'Morning,' I reply, my voice steady. 'Hop on.'

He frowns at the bike, but puts his cup on the windowsill and zips up his jacket. 'Just – on?'

I pat the raised ridge behind my seat, the size of two hands and lightly padded. Not exactly a passenger seat, but it works. At least, I imagine it will. I've seen other people doing it, but I've never had a passenger. He climbs on. For a second I think he's going to wrap his arms around my waist, like a girl in a film. But he puts his hands behind him and grips the metal casing over the back tyre.

'Ready?' I ask.

'Steady,' he replies, the heat of his breath right on my ear. The boat dips into a swell and my stomach lurches and I look for the horizon, then remember that we're not on the boat yet. I check the handlebars, check the ignition, check the front tyre. Finally I dare to take my feet off the ground.

At the passing place I stop the bike. I hand Tom my spare water-proofs. We pull them on in silence. This early, it's just us and the birds. We slither down the rocks and into the motorboat. Without my directions, Tom settles amongst the crates, perfectly balanced. The motor rrr-rrr-hhhrrrrs and I steer us through the milky-cool mist. Below the wheeling bonxies, past the rolling lolling seals, out towards the pinkish-grey sky. I anchor the motorboat and we step aboard the fishing boat.

I have to concentrate. There's the vivier tank to set up, the engine to start, the winch to check. And there's Tom. Tom Flinch, on my boat.

'Where shall I stand?' he asks. His eyes are bright now, his lungs full of the cold morning air. That tuft of hair is sticking up at his crown.

'Oh,' I say, 'I don't know – anywhere, really. I've never had anyone out on the fishing boat before.'

'Well, I've never been on a fishing boat, so we're even.' He stands between the wheelhouse and the vivier tank, and I haven't told him to stand there but now I think about it, it's the perfect place.

The sea is flat calm, ideal fishing weather. I haul creels, open them, empty them, rebait them, stack them, reshoot them from the deck. There's no need to say *excuse me*, or instruct Tom to move. He watches me carefully, as if memorising my movements. His own body sways and shifts just when I need it to. We never bump or clash. I slip into my rhythm, and soon I'm moving from habit, my thoughts rising up, scattered and free. It's almost as though Tom isn't there, but not quite. As I work, the wind rises, kicking up white waves.

And then my fleets are all emptied. It's time to start the real work. I look over at Tom. I read his eyes the way I read the sea. Seeing when it's safe to go further out, and when it's better to head home. Knowing when it's just enough.

Don't take more than you need. But I need this.

I step towards Tom, and he doesn't step back. The waves lift and lower the boat. To keep our balance we lean forwards and back in rhythm. The boat tilts port, and I lean towards Tom while he leans away from me. It tilts starboard, and he leans in to me, and I have to lean away to keep from falling. A strange, seagoing dance.

'I have to tell you something,' I say.

'All right,' he replies. 'Is it about the catch?'

'No,' I say.

'Is it about the Inn?'

'No.'

'Is it . . .' He blinks and looks away, suddenly shy. 'Is it . . .'

The boat tilts starboard and Tom leans in to me. Instead of swaying away, I lean in. I kiss him. After a second, the boat tilts port and we both lean, together, lips pressed. I pull away and Tom smiles at me.

'James,' he says, 'James, I want –'

'Wait. There's something else,' I say. I look off the back of the boat, to the choppy pewter sea. Then I reach down and pull off my boots. My toes stretch to grip the deck. I dive in.

Ruth:

I'm going to tell you a story that I've heard many times. My granny told me it after my great-grampa died, and my aunt after my uncle died, and the man at the post office after his daughter died. They all told it the exact same way, although I asked them all differently. I wanted to know about their grief. I needed to know how it felt. I knew that it would come for me eventually and I needed to know how to manage it. I wanted to be ready.

I thought grief might feel like being always full of cold water. I thought it might feel like inside your body there's an empty space that's bigger than your body. Then I thought maybe it was cold black pebbles in your belly, or a grey cloud stuffed in your head, or a soft heavy weight always pressing down on your shoulders. I wanted a step-by-step process, so that I could get through it as quickly as possible and go back to normal. Start living my life again. So they told me, and I didn't understand. I was angry at them because I didn't understand their story.

Then, after my dad and my granddad died and I knew grief for myself, I realised that my granny, and my aunt, and the man in the post office had all told their story the best way they could. And now I could tell that story too. It won't make sense to you now, but someday it will. I hope that day will not come for a long time, but I am telling you now to prepare you. You must listen very carefully.

7
The Exact Sound of Grief

'

'

Liska:

Hello, nighttime! Hello, my little black hole! Hush now, stop consuming everything, stop expanding for a moment. It's time for a story. I know, I know, the night is noisy. Don't be afraid. The storm rises on its hind legs, bats our tiny house in its paws – but the smaller a mouse is, the more likely it is to escape. Here, we slip through the cracks of the world.

I want you to know, my darkness, that I don't like hiding this from your mama. We don't lie to one another. But still I must tell you these tales in secret, in the snoozing midnight, so she doesn't know. We agreed that stories are not truth, and that we'd never lie to you. But I've thought and thought, but there's no other way to give you the truth except to hide it in a story and let you find your own way inside. All stories contain a truth if you look hard enough – but it might not be a good truth.

This is a story I heard from my big sister, Anna. Like my other sister's story, it's a cruel one. And I promise that your life will be full of bright and pretty stories, but life must be more than that. It's only in darkness that we can appreciate light. I know that Anna is so excited to meet you, but you must be patient. She has her own sadnesses. You will grow bright, but one light does not get rid of all the world's dark.

8
Stars, Witch, Bear

I woke again to a cold bed. The morning was my aching eyes and the mist not yet burned off the trees. I stumbled sleepy to the reading chair and fell straight into stories. Forests and witches. Goblins and castles. Children who leave home to vanquish wicked creatures and return years later with their hands full of love and good fortune. Happy ever after.

My husband came home from his pre-dawn walk just as I was slotting toast between the tarnished ribs of the toast-rack. He hung up his overcoat and brushed at the sleeves. His palms came away wet with dew. When he sat beside me the scent of pinesap and cold air rose from his collar. He tugged a fistful of photos from his pocket and spread them across the marmalade-sticky table. The kitchen lights were too bright. They obscured our children's faces.

He said: 'I didn't find anything. No one in the city has seen them.'

I pushed a plate of eggs towards him. 'You tried. Perhaps no one has seen them because they're not there.'

'But I still feel them. I feel them in – ' He sat down and pressed a hand to his chest. 'How much time do we need? How long will it take to forget?'

'I don't know.' Did he think I didn't feel them too? Their loss weighed heavy between my ribs. 'There must be something wrong with the way we're looking. We'll never find an answer this way. We'll never forget if we don't find out who –' but he was pawing through the photos and not listening. I let the rest of my sentence fall away.

I didn't speak again for the rest of the day. The next morning was a cold bed, my aching eyes, the reading chair. The toast in the toast-rack.

He got back from his walk and said: 'I didn't find anything.' I didn't reply. He wouldn't hear anyway. Another day of silence.

On the third morning – which was really the previous night as it was long before dawn – on that morning I got up before my husband. There was no toast and no stories. I washed and dressed and packed a suitcase. I wanted to say to my husband: You can't forget if you don't have an ending. You can't let go of an unanswered question. Instead I called to him on my way out: 'You don't have to search today. I'm going instead.'

To one side of the house wound the road to town that my husband walked every night. To the other spread the woods. My husband had never walked that road. We'd always warned our children about the wicked witch at the heart of the woods – her sharp teeth and her gingerbread house and her fondness for eating sons for supper and daughters for dessert. That's why my husband searched the city. He thought that our children would have heeded our warnings.

But then I remembered my shelf of storybooks full of forests and castles and brave witch-vanquishing children. I realised that in my children's minds there would be no point in questing to the safeness of the city. My husband and I never spun tales of the city's dangers.

No one ever won treasure by following the well-trodden route. I walked off the path and into the trees.

Walking took up the rest of the day. I had thought that walking would let me notice the tracks my children left. But nature is not friendly and it took all my attention not to let it trip me or scrape me or tumble me down a hill. I had imagined myself the heroine of a fairytale – skin luminous with dew and robins alighting on my palms. But there were invisible midges in the murk beneath the trees that bit a rose-red rash on my forearms and chest. As I walked I rubbed my jaw on my shoulder to relieve the itch.

Hours passed. I began to see the ghosts of my children in every tree branch. At first I rushed towards them but then I saw they were only shadows. My calves were tense as logs and my belly was shrunken and gnawing. I put my suitcase at the base of a tree and sat on it. Behind me lay a spread of photos on a sticky table and the syrupy tick of the clock. A house unforgetful with questions. Why had our children left? And why had they not come back? Before me lay answers – if I could learn to see them. I leaned my head against the tree-trunk and closed my eyes.

I woke to an orchestra of insects. It was so dark that for a moment I thought I still had my eyes shut. It took me a while to realise that I had slipped onto my side and that my cheek was on something soft. I lay still and blinked while I waited for my eyes to adjust to the moonlight. I soon realised that there was no moonlight and so my eyes were useless. My hand stretched out into the blind dark.

Something giving and dense like my hair after I haven't washed it for a week.

Something hard and smooth and curved; bigger than a fist and tapered to a point.

It was the paw of a bear and it was under my head. The insects still ached at my ears and I shifted so that I was sitting upright – slowly so as not to wake the bear. I swayed with dizziness. In the dark it was impossible to know his size or his pose or his intentions. If I wanted I could have followed the bear's paw along the line of his leg to his body to see how big he was.

I did not want to know how big he was. I wanted a cold bed and the syrupy tick of the clock. But my bed had been made for me – and it had claws.

There would be no use in running. I was a day's walk from home. If I ran the bear would chase me and he would eat me.

In the absence of a better plan I lay back down and spent the night motionless with my cheek on the bear's waxy paw. Morning came and I found that the bear had not eaten me. I also found that he was a she. She lumbered into the shadows and returned with a breakfast of berries and silver birch bark. We ate and stretched. We shat and then buried it. We began the search.

Together the bear and I were silent ramshackle police as we fingertip-searched the forest floor: she for food and me for signs of my children. That first day she was successful and I was not. But the next day came soon enough.

The days congealed into weeks. Together the bear and I made a new home. No roof. No furniture. Just the outline of a house clawed in the ground. The forest unfolded under our feet as we searched. She found everything: squirrels grass bees fish mushrooms acorns. Enough to fill our bellies every night. I found nothing and nothing and nothing.

After a time I came to see that the bear was not just searching for food. She was searching for her children too. Such a neat story. Two mothers united in their search. I couldn't have written it any neater if I'd made it up.

But it was not enough. We weren't finding anything. I had educated my children on stories and that taught me to expect satisfactory endings. The bear was not giving me an ending.

One morning I ate my last breakfast of blackberries and mouse-flesh with the bear then carefully explained to her that I was leaving. She did not reply because she was a bear. I shouted at her to go away. She did not shout back because she was a bear. I pulled a handful of thorns from a bush and hit her – half the thorns pressed back into my palm and the other half disappeared into her thick fur. She reared up and pushed meaty breath into my face. Her teeth were bright as bones. This was the moment that she would leave me or eat me.

She thudded back down. Then she turned and padded away with her paws kicking up scoops of dead leaves. Lulled by the slow beat of the bear's retreating paws I lay down and let the afternoon sun warm my face.

I woke with the stars nipping bright at my eyelids. I lay still and watched them tell me stories. There among the constellations I could find all my answers if I looked long enough. People did that. Didn't they? Told the future and the past from the stars? In all my time with the bear I had never looked up.

I began a new rhythm. Sleeping daylight away curled in the hollow base of a dead tree. Spending the nights watching and reading and listening and learning. I saw my children living in the city and working in shops and bars and drinking and laughing so wide the light gleamed off their wisdom teeth. I saw my children living on a boat in the middle of the sea and eating fish and seaweed and hunting for adventure. I saw my children living in a house not unlike my own with their own children – ones that would not leave. I saw my children living.

Sometimes my stomach made noises or pains to remind me to eat. I chewed leaves and bark. I didn't want to look away from the sky to find berries. Even standing and even in daylight I couldn't stop looking at the sky. My head was always tilted back with my throat stretched tight. I forgot to blink.

Every day brought a new story of my children. A new ending. A new answer. As the stories increased I didn't know which to believe. They couldn't all be true and if only one was true then the others were lies. And if one was a lie then they could all be lies.

I could have stayed in my new home among the stars. I could have become an astrologer or a soothsayer collecting conclusions to share with other lost people. But all the stories I had seen in the stars were just things I had made up. They weren't answers.

Still staring at the sky I blinked. Then I blinked again. There was something caught in my eye. I lowered my head and felt my neck crack and my vertebrae separate. Looking away from the sky made me dizzy.

I rubbed my eyes and looked at what was left on my fingertips. It was snowing tiny flecks of gingerbread. It reeked of sugar and spice and witches. The witch from the storybooks. The one that brave children always vanquished. I had forgotten about her.

I turned away from the sky and looked instead to the forest floor. I ran. Branches whipped my forehead and bruised my shoulders but I didn't stop until I reached the furthest-away part of the woods. I stopped.

A grassy clearing in a patch of sun. A siren of birdsong. A house with gingerbread walls and sugarpaned windows and a gumdrop doorknob and it looked just like the ones in the stories I'd read every night to my children – and the doorknob turned, and the door opened. I was winded and couldn't get my breath and couldn't move and couldn't run but it was okay because it was just an old lady. An old lady in a house made of sweets and nothing could be safer than that. The lady leaned out of her front door without putting her feet over the threshold.

'I have answers in here for you. My dear. My dear. I have answers.' Her voice was like caramel.

This was a story I had read before and I knew that she was the ending. She couldn't seem to step over the threshold so I walked around her house and her garden and her roof and her walls and her windows to try to find a way inside.

I found nothing and nothing and nothing. The lady stayed in the doorway saying reassuring things. But by the time I'd made it around the house my imagination couldn't hold her properly. Her words blurred and smudged. Her eyes dripped down her cheeks like melted chocolate. Her teeth grew through the flesh of her chin and upper lip. They were sharp as snapped toffee. I had imagined her as my perfect ending. The story conclusion I needed. But she was the least real thing I had ever seen.

I blinked and the gingerbread house disappeared. I stood alone in the clearing.

My skin still smelled of the bear's fur and the bear's nose and the bear's saliva. All those months of searching with her and eating with her and watching her eat any living thing that could fit between her paws – and still I did not see. I was blinded by the wicked witch I'd grown in my imagination and fed on storybooks.

I'd thought the bear was a mother like me. I'd thought the opposite of a mother was a scary old child-eating hag hiding away in the woods. But I was wrong: the bear was not like me. She was a bear. I had ignored the scraps of my runaway children caught between her teeth.

The cruellest things do not hide in the dark. They sit in full view in the sunlight and in the clearings. I had found an ending. But I did not want it.

I walked to the edge of the forest. Sacrificial and willing. Looking for the bear's jaws. But she had gone. Perhaps she had found her cubs and her ending. Instead I turned and walked back home. I found my house exactly where I left it. In the kitchen was my husband. He was still sitting at the table which was still covered in photos which were now marmalade-sticky.

He said: 'Did you find them?'

'Yes.' I took his hand and pulled him away from the photos. Together we settled into the reading chair. It was big enough for both of us. 'I found them.'

'Will they come back?'

I said: 'No. That's not how the story goes. Let me tell you the ending.'

He closed his eyes and settled into the chair. I would tell him stories: our children living in the city with light gleaming off their wisdom teeth. Our children living on a boat and hunting for adventure. Our children living.

One day when my husband was ready I would take him into the woods. I would show him the real ending. But not yet. I could no longer have the comfort of stories – but he could. I settled in beside him and began a new story.

Ruth:

Sometimes I want to shelter you here forever, Coorie. I can keep you safe inside me – but how can I keep you safe when you're out there in the world? You'll make your choices, I know you will. And they'll be right for you, because there's no such thing as a wrong decision. Everything we do – everything we choose – makes us who we are. Every setback, every hurt feeling, every wrong thing we ever do helps us to grow. So you must never regret, my Coorie. You must own your choices. Know that we will love you whatever you choose.

This is a story that my dad told me. I'm sorry to say that you can never meet him, because he'd gone out of this world before you were in it. If you listen carefully, you'll hear that I'm in this story too. It's strange to hear a story about yourself, to understand yourself as a character – strange to realise that your whole life is only a bit part in other people's narratives. But so it is.

Maybe someday I'll take you to Arran. Maybe you'll choose the same path as I did, or as my dad did, or as my granddad did – or maybe you'll find a new path entirely. Whatever you choose, my Coorie, it will be right for you. I wish my dad had realised that sooner – but that is why I am telling you his story.

9

Cold Enough to Start Fires

I didn't find it. I didn't find it in books or booze. I didn't find it in my wife's arms, or in her vows, or in her screaming spread mouth as she cursed me to hell while pushing out our firstborn. I didn't find it between school and university, summering as a kitchen porter on a cruise liner, stumbling out of my teens and half-drunk with triple-shift exhaustion on the deck of the snoring boat under a sky scribbled with seagulls. I didn't find it in the messy kisses of girls in back gardens or behind bike-sheds or sweating in the sheets of my student digs or, once, high and dared at a party, with my best friend Tom. I didn't find it as I watched my father die, huddled around the hospital bed with my two brothers, our fists clenched as he wheezed through cancerous lungs, his final breath a half-completed inhalation. But I'm getting ahead of myself. First I must tell you what I was searching for.

I was thirteen that summer. I was small – you would have thought I was nine or ten. In those sweat-blurred and endless days I had only two desires: to see my father do one kind thing for my mother, and to hide. We were holidaying on Arran: my father, mother, and two brothers. The first morning, my mother prepared breakfast before we woke and then retreated back to her bedroom, leaving us males to eat in awkward silence. My father emptied his plate, face obscured behind his newspaper, then stood up and announced grandly that he was driving to the shop and wouldn't be back for some time. I slipped away from the table and into the hall. If I held my breath, I could hear my mother's faint sobs through the closed door. I ran out after my father, not daring to shout or wave my arms, but bold enough to silently chase his car as it escaped down the driveway. I'm sure he saw me in his rear-view mirror. As I turned to go back inside, I glanced up at my mother's bedroom window. She didn't see me; she was looking at the retreating car. Though her face was swollen with tears, she was still as lovely as a painting. The air was calm and heavy with heat. The pale dust kicked up by the wheels of my father's car lurked ghostly for hours. I spent the rest of the day in piles of rotting leaves, their centres still crinkled, edges softening to damp. My clothes reeked of mulch. My hair itched with stalks. My father came home as dark fell, his hair tousled and his temper quick.

From then on, each day repeated just the same. I only let myself be seen at mealtimes, when I'd perch on the edge of my chair and talk in shrugs. Every evening after dinner my mother served up fresh berries and cream with her head bent and shoulders hunched; every night my brothers snatched my bowl and divided the spoils amongst themselves, with my father looking on in approval. I'd asked him before why he didn't help me; why he didn't make my brothers share with me. *I am helping you*, he'd reply. *You need more fire in you.* After several repetitions, I stopped asking him why. I stopped asking him anything at all. My silence meant that my father had to search hard for reasons to discipline me; but my brothers helped, gleeful that

I was so convenient a scapegoat for every smashed window and broken-winged bird. The best part of the day was each night, when I adventured alone in bed, reading books under the covers with a candle. It's a wonder I didn't set the place alight. Perhaps if I had, then – but no. It did not happen, and I will not tell you lies.

For the first week I managed to hide, but soon Gordon and Michael found my den. They shrieked with glee as they threw lit matches into my leaf-pile, crowing that they'd found the villain and now he would pay. They'd been reading spy novels, casting themselves as joint hero and speaking in code, but they ensured my nickname – Inbetweener – was obvious enough. You might think that being the middle brother would mean I was closest to both of them, but it didn't work that way; instead, being in the middle meant I was always the piggy. I limped away from the leaf-pile, scalp throbbing but with no blood shed. A mile from the house, the path split. The south fork still held the dusty ghost of my father's exit. I chose the north fork. I walked for hours. The air was so still that it only seemed to move when I inhaled it. Finally, when my head had started to spin, I crested a hill and found the lochan. I ran downhill so fast I almost toppled into the water. At its edges the water was so clear I could barely see the line where it licked the shore. But the centre was deep and dark. I dipped my face and hands into the edges, the water so cold it took my breath.

On the grassy banks I lay out like a sultan. I'd been reading Biggles books and the baddies were always coffee-skinned with heavy accents, draped in rich cloths and sensual women. Who'd give a fig for flying goggles when you could have that? My knuckles were skinned from a week's worth of brotherly fighting so I picked at the scabs and let the thin drops of blood pool in the hollows between my bones, pretending it was rubies. I sneaked glances at the lochan. It scared and fascinated me. There was an algae-choked chain attached to the rocks, leading into the water. I decided it was for a dragon. An ancient beast, long dormant, shifting its sleeping feet on a stack of crowns and coins. My father said I needed fire – well, I'd bring the dragon home and set the whole house alight.

Hours passed. The air was dusty, my knuckles ached. The longer I lay there the more the realisation sank in: I wasn't the sultan. My father was. He was the lord of us all; he decided when we would be disciplined and when rewarded; when it was time to go away and when to stay. He moved freely through the world in a way that none of us could. And where was he now? Off with his harem, laughing over foreign cigars, telling his women that he had two strong and powerful sons, and no other children, no weak and scrawny boy hiding in a leaf pile. I wished he were here so I could drown him in the pool. I knew I would never be like him. I would have a wife and children, and I would love them, and I would be kind to them, and the fire of the love they gave back would keep me warm. I would never leave them. They would be everything to me. Anger burned. My skin throbbed with heat. But the water was dark as animals' eyes; at its centre, it reflected nothing. My fear pushed me into the water. I resolved to stay at the clear edges – but surely the water in the centre was the same as that at the edges, but just in greater quantity? I took a step. And another. My body resisted but I pushed it onward. Before I knew it, I'd waded right into the centre of the lochan, the water chilling up my legs to my belly to my chest. As I walked the rocks jabbed into my feet, until suddenly they didn't. A stream of bubbles emerged near me, and I knew – I just knew – that it was the dragon awakening. Under the water where I couldn't see, it was opening its jaws wider, wider, and my kicking feet looked so delicious . . .

My imagination flipped open the top of my head like a steam whistle, and all my fears came blasting out. Panic choked me. Through the haze of my splashing, far away on the shore, I saw that the stones were speckled with my blood. I sank down further until the water closed over my head and I had to swallow or choke, so I swallowed.

Down –

down –

shadowed velvet depths –

soft licks –

numb skin tingling –

light turns pink –

red –

black –

fingers to lips –

legs around waist –

bony hands on my backside –

pushed up up up cork from a bottle –

hard shale of shore under my knees –

air around me–

sky above me. Breathe.

Breathe.

I crawled free of the water. I was sick, dramatically, followed by noisy retching. With my wrist I rubbed at my eyes until they were dry, then crawled back to the lochan to scoop water into my mouth, rinse, then spit it back out onto the stones. It was only then that I looked up. And then – well, it's difficult to explain. It couldn't have been a dragon, of course, because we all know that dragons don't exist, but it was . . . something. If my childish mind perceived it as a dragon, then that is simply because I had no closer points of reference at the time. Memory, too, can play tricks. A dragon was the closest thing I can describe, but it seemed wrong somehow; it loomed huge against the sky, but its teeth were broken, its eyes pale as dust. *You will have what you need* – the dragon spoke in a voice sharp as smashing dishes – *You will have your fires.*

When I came back to myself, I was hunched over the bramble bushes at the point where the path split north and south, frantically grabbing at the overripe berries. My handkerchief was already filled with fruit, so I tied its corners and threw it on the ground. Burst berries blooded the tartan. Still I couldn't stop: fistfuls of berries, more and more, falling off the branch and into my hands. Every time I added a berry, another fell from my grasp and plopped on my still-damp shoes. My handkerchief overflowed, and I began to fill the pockets of my shorts, the fruit soft and warm against my thighs. I imagined their juice seeping through the fabric and onto my skin, red as rubies. Finally I stopped when the weight of the berries on top of my collection was crushing those at the bottom into pulp. I turned towards the house. I remember noting that the ghost of my father's car had fallen from the southern fork. As I trudged up the path, Michael emerged from one of my abandoned leaf-piles.

'Inbetweener!' he crowed. 'Glorry me yom pickingnicks.'

I played at hiding the berries from him, while letting the corner of the handkerchief fall back to reveal its juicy contents. It didn't matter if he took them all. My pockets bled with fruit, enough for a whole world of greedy brothers.

'Berries!' he crowed, forgetting his secret language.

He reached for them greedily, then looked up at my face. Whatever he saw there made him pause. He looked at me for a long time.

'No,' he said. 'I don't want them.'

'Whyever not?' I tried to seem reluctant, but I could feel the flames flickering behind my eyes.

'Father said not to eat berries unless you know what they are.'

'They're blackberries. Any fool can see that.'

'They look funny.'

'That's not really why. Go on, take them. I won't stop you.'

'No. I don't want them.'

I shrugged. 'Suit yourself.'

I sat cross-legged, out in the open among the scattered leaf-piles, and ate all the blackberries. They were delicious. I saw now that I did not have to be a bully like my brothers, and I did not have to hide like my mother. I had searched, and I had found the answer. I could have everything, and I did not have to give up anything to get it. I left the berries' bloody juice on my chin so that my brothers could see how much I'd enjoyed them.

Childhood passed. Every summer we returned to Arran; every summer my father drove away to what I eventually realised was the house of his mistress, leaving his ghost above the south fork; every summer I stayed away from both paths. I had already earned my fire and I did not need to prove myself again. I pretended that my father was a ghost, long dead, and that his physical presence was nothing more than madness on my part. He followed suit, looking through me rather than at me, and my knuckles never bled again. I refused to be piggy-in-the-middle any longer, and instead I took my proper place between my brothers. Perhaps 'took' is not a strong enough word, for I feel that I seized my place, demanded it, as a usurping king does a throne. Granted, I would never be the high-achieving eldest like Michael, carving out a path for the others to follow; nor the cherished youngest like Gordon, forgiven for tantrums and always given first choice of cake. That is probably why, twenty years later when my own son was born, I nicknamed him Goldenboy. But I am getting ahead of myself. Before the boy came the girl: my dreamy, manipulative Tuppence, eyes the blue of cornflowers and a foot that could stamp hard enough to shake the world. Netty and I stopped at two. I would never bring an Inbetweener into the world.

But again, I am rushing ahead. When we had entered secondary school, Mother decided that Michael was to be a university professor, Gordon was to be a lawyer, and I was to be a doctor. I would do anything to make her happy, and got through the biology undergraduate with a First from St. Andrews. But six months into my first MB, Gordon dropped out of law school to sail around the world, and Michael gave away all his possessions and went to live in a commune in America. Trying to fix them consumed my mother entirely, and her weekly phone calls to me dwindled to six-monthly letters. Just before I dropped out of my MB I met Natasha – my Netty, as she soon came to be. I wrote poems about her and recited them as we ventured across the rainy beaches of St. Andrews; when the poems would not come, I scoured anthologies of others' words and printed her initials next to the ones that reminded me of her. In her wellies and huge owl-eyed glasses, wind whipping wild through her hair, she was the most beautiful woman in the world. She had quick hands and a slow smile. She was clever, but elegant enough to wear her cleverness lightly. There were not enough words for me to tell her how much I loved her.

The next decade was swallowed up by the flower-child wedding, the jobs in pharmaceuticals (me) and a university library (Netty), the move to a snoozing village in Yorkshire, and the carefully planned creations of Tuppence and Goldenboy. Tuppence loved dressing up, spaghetti carbonara, climbing up the slide, pottering, and hitting Goldenboy. Goldenboy loved balloons, stroking the cat's tail, apple slices, and hitting Tuppence back. Every time I looked at my children my stomach contracted with joy and fear. In the years after the children were born, Netty and I had became strangely lonely. We were brought together by our children, but separated by them too. The teddy bear picnics, the smell of warm skin, dancing around to the plink-plunking of the piano after baths, tales of tomorrow and dreams of yesterday. How very busy we were. Every morning I resolved to connect with Netty, to talk with her the way we used to – but buggies must be pushed, shells collected, sibling ceasefires brokered. By the time we'd done the dinner-bath-bed ritual, I could never think of a single thing to say to her. I did not write anyone's initials in margins, because the only books I read were about Burglar Bill and the Very Hungry Caterpillar. And so the years piled up and the fires dampened down. It became clear that the sparks I'd felt in childhood had not caught, but had sputtered to nothing. I had tried to lay it right, with all the proper structures – the firelighter of my marriage, the kindling of my work, the sparked match of my children – but it did not keep me warm. I waited for my bliss to arrive. I waited to wake up every day glorying in the joy of achieving all my goals. But I could not wait for ever. I wished for more.

The summer that Tuppence was nine and Goldenboy four, I suggested a trip to Arran. We could not afford to rent the same house that I'd stayed in as a child, but this one had the same dusty, holiday-house smell: the stack of board games below the TV; the shelf of abandoned paperbacks; mini packets of cornflakes in the kitchen cupboards. The first few days of the trip passed like any other. We could have been in any seaside town in the world: beaches, ice creams, and sun-grumpy children. A Wednesday afternoon, halfway through our holiday, I chanced my escape. The children had played themselves to snoozing in the shady garden and Netty was deeply into a paperback thriller, a glass of something icy balanced on her knee. On holiday, she remained unperturbed by tantrums and unfinished dinners and intra-child thumps, because Daddy was sorting it out, wasn't he? I mumbled something about going for a walk and slipped away.

At the point where the paths diverged, no ghost hung over the south fork. Where the brambles had proliferated, now there stood a greenhouse. Some of the panes were incomplete, shattered by mischief, and those remaining were opaque with dirt. I chose the north fork. The lochan, at least, was unchanged. Grassy banks and an algae-choked chain attached to the rocks; clear edges, a dark centre. I fell into a doze. In my dreams, the dragon emerged. It no longer loomed huge. Now that I looked closely, it seemed no larger than a man, albeit a rather tall man. More of its teeth were broken, and the jagged edges flashed sun at me. Its dusty eyes blinked once, then closed.

I'm here about the fires, I said.

Ahhhh, sighed the dragon in understanding.

They didn't start, I said.

You mean that you did not start them. Fires do not begin from nothing.

I thought of sun on parched forests, light through glass; but thought it best not to argue.

Your father knew sparks, said the dragon. *There was so much fire in him that his eyes burned red.*

I never want to be my father, I said.

If dragons could shrug, that's what it did.

Should I have chosen the south fork? I asked. *Should I have made Michael and Gordon eat the berries? Should I have become a doctor? Should I have had the kids later? Earlier? Should I have married someone else? Should I have asked for more? Demanded more? Should I have –*

It wouldn't have mattered, said the dragon. *We don't choose what we are, just what we are not.*

This was not what I wanted to hear. I remembered that I was listening to a dragon, and that I was dreaming, and that both dragons and dreams weren't real. Then the dragon was not there, and I was awake.

I woke inside the greenhouse at the split of the paths. From ground to roof it was stuffed with fat tomatoes. The scent was overwhelming: sparking fresh and sweet with juice. Across my feet crawled a proliferation of ladybirds. I pulled my tartan handkerchief from my pocket. I thought perhaps I would bring some tomatoes back for dinner – I would have to hide them in a spag bol for Tuppence and

Goldenboy, but I would save the two plumpest to slice neatly and feed raw to Netty after dark, her eyes caught in mine, our heads dizzy with wine. If I acted like a happy and fulfilled man, then I would be a happy and fulfilled man. I reached for the nearest tomato, but then I tucked the handkerchief back into my pocket. Why should I share? I had spent my life sharing, eating other people's burnt crusts, waiting for the last sip of water, parcelling out joy so that only a sliver was left for me. Why shouldn't I have everything I wanted, even if I had to take it from someone else? Everything, and more. I would eat the tomatoes myself. I would eat them until I made myself sick. With both hands I reached out. The tomato burst over my fingers, its taut skin containing only liquid, overripe and rotten. Stench rose around me. In a daze I reached for another tomato. It burst across my hands – and another, and another. I flung out both arms and tore down the fat whiskery vines, tomatoes squashing to pulp beneath my feet. Rotten, every one of them rotten.

I emerged, panting and blinking. The sun beat bright and white into my eyes. My head throbbed. I would take the other path. It wasn't too late. My father had taken that path, and he had been a lot of things, things I hadn't thought I wanted to be. But he had never seemed unhappy. I took the south fork. I was ready to walk for hours, but I'd barely broken a sweat when I rounded a corner and came upon a pool. My mind struggled over the puzzle: trying to see a geometric shape from another angle, figuring which parts fitted together. I felt the shock of the unexpectedly familiar. This was not a pool. This was *my* pool, with my dragon. Both paths led to – the south was a shorter way to – I felt sick. From this shore the pool did not seem so treacherous. There were no sharp stones or steep angles.

The water looked inviting. But I did not feel hot. The sweat chilled on my forehead and I held back a shiver. I turned away from the pool and walked back along the south fork. As I rounded the hill by the greenhouse, I stopped and ducked back into the shadows.

Tuppence approached along on the path. The air was still. I crouched behind the hill, spying on her from the darkness. My baby girl, my firstborn child, my much-maligned angel, the writer of her own destiny. She would make her choices, as I had made mine. I bowed my head. Whichever fork she chose, it wouldn't matter. Both led to the same awful place. I could not bear to watch.

I heard the scuff of her feet on the ground.

'Dad!' she called. 'Daddy, where are you?'

I saw myself, silently chasing my father's car, not daring to shout for him. I saw the dusty ghost that lurked after he'd gone.

'I'm here!' I stumbled as I emerged from the hill's shadow. 'I'm here, Tuppence.'

I swooped my hands to my daughter's waist and lifted her up onto my shoulders. Her cry of surprise became a shout of laughter. She pressed her hands to the top of my head for balance. At nine, she was far too old to be carried on my shoulders; her gangly legs hung down over my chest, her sandaled heels thumping against my ribs.

She bent to whisper in my ear. 'I came to find you.'

'I know,' I said. 'And you found me.'

'Come on, horsey.' She bumped her feet against me, cracking imaginary reins. 'Let's go home.'

And we did.

Liska:

Hello, little fire! How I've missed you. Sometimes I think that everything outside this house is just a story – and you and me and your mama, that's the truth hidden inside the story. Now, you must be good and quiet so I can tell you tonight's tale. It's a sad one, but I think you'll like it.

Before I begin, do you see this statue? Yes, I know you can't see it yet, so you must imagine. This is Mary. Your mama keeps Mary here, on this table beside our bed, to watch over us. Remember I introduced you to my troll? Your mama thinks he is ugly, a silly folk superstition. I think the same about her Mary, but still I let her watch over us. We all need to believe that someone will look after our children when we can't.

It hurts me to say, but there were others before you. Other little clams who couldn't hold on to the shore when the tide went out. This has been the story for many people in the past, and it will be for many people still to come. That's partly why we came here, to this little sea-house – the quiet, the calm. Your mama thought it might help you to hold on. I hope you will never know the sadness of such loss, my summer snowflake. But if you ever do, I hope this story will help you as it helped me.

This is a very old story I heard from my grandmamma, though it was not hers. It's such an old story that it belongs to everyone. It was told to her, and she told it to me, and now I'm telling it to you.

10
The Mother of Giants

"Once upon a time, there was a little boy who thought he was cleverer than everyone else. To prove it, he crept away from his mother and father to the darkest part of the woods. He felt cold claws grip his shoulder. 'What boy dares to trespass on my land?' hissed the witch in a voice like ice . . ."

"Witch witch witch. Whisper her name and feel the freezing wind blow through your ribs. She'll boil up your eyes for sausages. She'll feed your fingers to her chickens. She's the only one who never starves. She can eat every single part of you because she's got iron teeth that can crunch–munch up your bones . . ."

"There was a woman who loved her baby. But love is not food, and no matter how hard she tried, she could not feed her child or herself. She despaired. But then she remembered an old story she had heard, a tale of someone who would take babies, and raise them big and fat and strong . . ."

Thirteen days after she'd made my little brother, my mother named him Robin. She waited those thirteen days to confuse the witch. If no one uses a name out loud, then the witch doesn't know that there's anyone new in the village, and she can't steal him away.

We didn't worry too much about the witch back then. We ate twice a day: when the sun came, and again when it left. After the first eating, the fathers tended to the crops and beasts, and the mothers wiped and fed and fussed over the babies.

I played at ghosts with the other children, creeping through the village in silent tiptoeing, trying to get through all the houses without being seen. We'd make necklaces from dried nuts or seedpods or discarded bird feathers – this was a challenge for a ghost, as the necklaces thudded and clacked with every movement. If the others were busy with chores, I was made busy too: scrubbing out pots with salt, throwing seed for chickens, collecting sticks for kindling in the lightest parts of the woods.

When the sun left, we ate again. Afterwards, full-bellied and wrapped in blankets, I nudged close to the fire, ready for stories. The dogs nosed around Robin, sniffing at the scent of new life. My mother wrapped my shoulders in the blankets and my hands around a cup of hot milk. 'Once upon a time', she said, and when she got to 'ever after' my head was nodding, my half-finished cup of milk tipping out of my hands. I wouldn't get in trouble for that – the cows were fat and broody, and we could have as much milk as we wanted. My mother tucked me in, kissed the top of my head, and tucked Robin's milk-dozy body in beside me. I pulled the blankets up over our heads. I wanted to whisper stories to him in the cave of our breath, but it was too hot. I pulled the blankets back and tucked them under his fat little chin. The wind howled at the shutters and the swooping yellow fire cast shadows around the house. Love pulsed through our home like blood through a good strong heart.

At the table, the fathers carved pipes and statues from wood, their voices burring like the growls of bears. Around the fire, the mothers knitted blankets and darned socks and checked on the babies, both named and unnamed. Their hands and eyes were always moving. When they thought I was asleep, they told stories about the safety of the village and the danger of the woods. The stories they told one another were similar to the stories my mother told me, but not the same. They told stories about the witch, because everyone told stories about the witch.

One girl, moony with love for her husband-to-be, had wandered too far into the dark part of the woods and was found two weeks later, half-mad, singing tunelessly to herself, her front teeth chipped as if she'd tried to bite down on metal. One man had become greedy, dissatisfied with his winter berries, sure that a sweeter crop grew on the other side of the shadows; he hadn't returned, but his clothing had been found torn and strewn among the high branches, his hunting knife plunged deep into a tree trunk. One boy had gone giggling into the woods on a dare, and stumbled home the following dawn with his right hand missing. The next night his finger bones, gnawed clean and sucked of marrow, were left in a stack at the edge of the village.

My dreams pulsed red and white and sharp, blood on snow and the flash of iron teeth. I woke up sobbing the witch's name, and after that the village mothers always told their stories too quietly for me to hear.

*

The witch did not get us. But hunger came for us instead. I don't know what happened to the food; I just know that, slowly and then all at once, there was none. We did not eat when the sun came, only when it left. Eating by the light of the fire meant we could see the shadows cast by the food and pretend it was bigger on the dish. Shadows couldn't be eaten, though, and my parents' meals were gone in two bites. Then they watched us eat from behind hooded eyes, pretending they weren't watching. Robin and I tried not to hunch over and cram food into our mouths as if worried that someone was about to steal it.

Food was all anyone thought about, though they never said. We saw it in our parents' tight smiles and shadowed eyes. Every night we ate, being regretted. Each stale crust and each quarter-egg, regretted. We made sure to chew every last crumb, and we licked our hands clean. I don't know if that made them regret us less or more. We feared our hunger, but it was hard to fear a lack, hard to fear a feeling inside your own body. Always, always, there was a greater and easier fear: the witch.

'Once upon a time', my mother said to us every bedtime. Robin and I pulled the blankets to our chins, sipping our thimbles of hot milk so it would last for the whole story. Robin was littler than me, and was still put to sleep by the lull of our mother's voice. When I was a child like him I'd always be dozing by the 'ever after'. I remembered all the milk I'd wasted. How I longed for it now.

One morning, we awoke to find that the village's newest baby – so new it had not even been named – was gone. How could the witch get him, I wondered, when no one had used his name? Her power must be growing the hungrier we got.

That night, the fathers clustered at our table, but they spoke only in nods. Instead of carving pipes, they carved tiny wooden totems, one by each man to represent the lost baby.

The mothers still huddled at the fire, endlessly knitting new blankets from the scraps of other worn-out blankets. The mother of the lost baby sat closest to the fire, clutching a handful of scraps and staring into the flames. The other mothers clustered around her. Their voices rose and fell like an uncertain storm, loud enough that a single exclamation pulled me from sleep, then quiet enough that I couldn't make out the words.

I started to pull the covers over my head, thinking that if I could not hear mention of the witch, she would not be able to find me – but my ears prickled. This was not the story of the witch. This was a new story. I held my breath, all the better to listen.

'There was a woman who loved her baby', announced one mother. By the firelight, I saw the other mothers look at her in surprise. Tentatively, another mother chimed in: 'But love is not food.' Another mother took up the tale, and then another, each adding a sentence as the story grew. 'And no matter how hard she tried, she could not feed her child or herself. She despaired. But then she remembered an old story she had heard. A tale of someone who would take babies, and raise them big and fat and strong.'

I wanted to hear this new story. But my bed was warm, and my brain was fogged with hunger, and the storm of voices dropped too quiet. Sleep crept in.

The witch lurked at the edge of the village, through snow-crunchy winters and slow-burning autumns. Through lost children and lost mothers and lost fathers. Through the slow deaths of the last of the cattle and the desperate slaughter of our chickens. Our meals were gone in a single bite. The fathers carved many more totems. These were gifted to the grieving families, who lined them up on the inside of their windowsills and never once complained that the statues were useless, being made of wood and no good for eating. Each time a baby disappeared, the mothers told the new story, though I never managed to hear the end.

Somehow, my mother began to grow fat. Her belly swelled like a summer cloud. Every part of her went to feed her belly: her eyes shrank in hollowed sockets, her arms thinned to string, her shoulders grew as sharp as chicken's beaks. But her belly ballooned. I imagined it full of milk, the milk that I no longer got at bedtime, the milk I'd wasted.

And then one day Robin was only my next-littlest brother, because my mother made Boy. Boy was the littlest in the village, now or ever. He was so little that my father could have hidden him in his closed-over hands. But you would have thought Boy was a giant for what it took from our mother to make him.

When we crept to her bed, for a moment we couldn't see her. Only one lamp was lit, and the blankets made a mass of shadows. We shuffled closer. Then a blanket moved, and we recognised our mother's face. She was as pale as new snow, even her hair and eyes. She reached out a hand to us and it looked like nothing so much as a bunch of silver birch twigs. Robin flinched back, and it took everything I had not to copy him. I tightened the muscles of my legs and leaned in to take the hand. It felt cold and hot: the fingertips icy, the palms slippery with sweat. My mother croaked my name, crow-like.

I leaned in to her, pressing my face to her scrawny neck, inhaling her comforting scent. I was so hungry that I would gladly have eaten her hair.

Our meal was potato roots and parings of bacon fat boiled in snow-water. Watching us sip it, my father clenched and unclenched his fists. I made the fatty chunks last, chewing each small mouthful as long as I could.

Afterwards I slid into bed without complaint, tucking the blanket up under Robin's chin. My mother was too weak to get out of her bed. Boy wriggled and squalled beside her. The mothers huddled around her bed, which was so surprising I almost opened my eyes. I had expected them to ignore Boy: new tiny people were the witch's favourite, and she was always listening. But instead they cooed over him, pinching his pale cheeks and waggling his spindly legs.

'I must feed him', croaked my mother. 'I can't lift him. Will you lift him? Lay him on his mother.'

'Hush now,' said the mothers. 'You are too ill to feed him.'

'Let me try.'

'We have tried. You have no milk. You must not worry – he'll be fine. The Mother of Giants will feed him soon enough.'

'No!' cried my mother. 'She doesn't need to take him. I can feed him . . . I can . . .'

But she couldn't manage any more words. The mothers leant over her bed.

'There was a woman who loved her baby,' they whispered in chorus. And when they'd finished their story and dozed off in their chairs, when an icy wind whined through the black trees and powdery snow sifted under everybody's doors, someone came to our sleeping house and took Boy away.

That night I slid obediently into bed. The sickly fire flickered over my closed eyelids. The knitting needles click-clacked. The fathers began carving wooden totems of Boy for us to line up on our windowsill.

'There was a woman who loved her baby,' the story began, and I dug my fingernails hard into my palms so I would stay awake. I needed to know the end of the story – who the Mother of Giants was, and why they told her story over and over.

But my mother turned her face to the wall and said, 'I don't want this story.'

'It will help,' urged the mothers.

'Stories can't help now,' said my mother. 'A story didn't take him.' Her sobs shook the bed, the floor, the house. The story was told anyway, louder than my mother's sobs. Finally the story was finished, and the house was quiet. The women dozed in their chairs, heads tipped back, laps warmed by their knitting.

I lay awake. Finally I knew the end of the story. The mothers took their babies into the woods and left them out in the snow, and then the Mother of Giants took them, and they lived forever in a sunny land of banquets and dances and happiness.

My body felt stiff and hot. I hated Boy. I hated all the babies who had gone with the Mother of Giants. Why not me? It wasn't fair. I wanted banquets.

I slid out of bed, careful not to wake Robin. I would come back and get him later, when I had convinced the Mother of Giants to take us even though we weren't babies. My bare feet flinched from the cold floor, so I slid them into my father's fur boots, which reached to the tops of my legs. I added his fur cape and hat, and I was covered from head to toe. I slid out of the snoring house.

Into the woods I crept and crept and crept. The shadows of birds watched me. I straightened my back and stopped creeping. I strode through the woods in my oversized furs, pretending I was not afraid. The Mother of Giants lived in the darkest part of the woods – but so did the witch.

I glanced behind me and saw a shadow slip behind a tree. My heart lurched. I crouched with my fists to my mouth.

Then the shadows resolved into a shape I recognised. Robin. He had followed me. As I'd taken the furs, Robin had none at all. His shadow shivered. I couldn't go any further. If Robin froze to death, even the Mother of Giants couldn't save him. I strode over like a giant in my father's boots and wrapped Robin in the fur cape. Together we left the woods.

Back at home, I tucked the blanket up to Robin's chin and slid in beside him. The cold was in my bones and I couldn't stop shivering. Robin had followed me into the woods – but the witch followed me back out. When I shut my eyes, she was there. She had filthy matted hair and shining gold eyes and long sharp fingers like a bird's talons. She rushed towards me and her mouth opened so wide that it split her head open to show her black bloody teeth.

I shrieked awake, and found that my mother was gone. Her body lay still in her bed, but she was not there. The mothers huddled round her bed, while my father stood silent in the corner, his jaw set.

Like the sacrifice that breaks a curse, my mother's death ended the famine. That day, the first green shoot poked through the snow.

A pair of rabbits bounded right up to our door, their necks snappable and their haunches fat. There was a little food, and then more, and more, and after a while we forgot how it felt to be hungry.

Ten winters passed, each milk-full and heavy with the scent of roasting pork. I had my own boys, two fat babies, each with bright black eyes and dark copper hair. I named them both straight away: Owl and Fox, to make them clever, to make them sly, to make them never go hungry.

I forgot all about the Mother of Giants. I would never need her to take my children, for I could give them everything they needed.

And yet. And yet. Slowly and then all at once, there was no food.

Now I grow fat with my third child. It swells and fidgets inside me, and I know I am growing a giant because everything in me is going to it. I feel my eyes shrink in hollowed sockets, my arms thin to string, my shoulders grow as sharp as chicken's beaks. My belly balloons. I feel myself disappearing into my bed, lost in the folds of my blanket.

The other mothers cluster around my bed, needles click-clacking.

'There was a woman who loved her baby,' said one. Another added: 'But love is not food.'

One by one, they tell me the story of the Mother of Giants, the same one I had overheard as a child. I lie in my bed, cold with horror. All my life I believed that Boy was living forever in a sunny land of banquets and dances and happiness. I knew that the mothers took their babies into the woods and left them out in the snow. I knew what they had done. And yet I did not truly know. I envied those children, left to die alone. I wanted to join them.

'How could they?' I say. 'The mothers, they –'

But I am speaking to a deaf room. The night is dark, and the other mothers have drifted off, chins to chests. I feel that I will never sleep again. I imagine my baby, weeks old, shrinking smaller and smaller. Its hollowed eyes. Its fragile bones. Its weak sobs.

Then I imagine my baby, birth-new and swaddled in snow, falling into a gentle sleep. Its time in this world so quick and kind that it will only ever know good things.

I know that feeding this child will kill me: haven't I seen enough women, empty of milk, the child at their breast too weak to cry? I'm no good to Owl and Fox if I'm dead. I know what I have to do. There is no witch to snatch my child. There is no Mother of Giants to save him.

I shake the other mothers awake. My voice sounds in a croak, but this doesn't matter. However long it takes, I will make them see that we do not need the Mother of Giants any more. We don't need stories, because there is no shame in the truth.

"Once there was a village of brave, wise, loving women. They were brave because they made hard decisions without the comfort of stories. They were wise because they knew when to give life, and when to take it. They were loving because they did what was best for their children."

Ruth:

How big you've grown, Coorie! It's not long now until we can meet. My skin is stretched so tender around you. It feels as thin as silk, scored with pink dashes. I feel like the house's walls can't contain me. I barely fit through doorways. The bedsprings creak every time I move. Bodies may be portable shelters, but I'm barely portable! I used to walk you along the shore so you could feel how the sea stretches out before us all the way to the top of the world. Now I can only just walk to the end of the garden path. I feel my hollow bones clatter and scrape as you grow. You started out so tiny that you were barely there at all: a pea hidden under a hundred mattresses. But even then I felt you there. You changed me.

There's not long now for me to finish my stories. But don't fret, because I only have a few left. Soon you'll be out in the world, and you can start making your own stories. But until then, let me finish telling you mine.

This is a story that my mum told me, slowly over many years. I think it took so long because it was so hard for her to tell. I'm not sure she understands it, even now. Once, long before I was born, when she had just left school, my mum married a man. They split up, and a year after that she met my dad, and a year after that they both met me. So let me tell you, Coorie. Let me tell you about how your mum's mum loved, and then didn't.

11
Small World

When the fairies steal human babies, they leave behind changelings.
These are ugly, misshapen and unhappy versions of the stolen child. As
well as children, the fairies occasionally also steal adults. Most vulner-
able are new brides, grooms and pregnant women.

STU: Do you want sugar? Here, use my spoon.

NAT: You're not listening.

STU: They don't have sweetener, only those sugar dispensers with the funnel in the top – and do you know, I once saw a child licking her finger and inserting it into the funnel? Over and over again she did it. I only take sugar if I'm at home now. Or if it's in those little paper sachets. More hygienic.

NAT: Stuart. Please listen.

STU: I'm not listening because this isn't you talking. I don't know who it is, but it's not you. Where's the woman I married? That woman was happy. That woman loved me.

NAT: It's still me. I can't help being unhappy.

STU: You have a husband. You have a home. What else could you possibly want?

NAT: See, that's the problem! There should be more.

STU: What should there be? What would make you happy?

NAT: I don't think – I don't know. That's what I'm trying to tell you.

STU: So do you want sugar or not?

NAT: I don't take sugar.

STU: You used to! You always used to.

NAT: Well. Now I don't.

Changelings are never happy. Some say that the happier the human was, the more miserable and angry their changeling will be. Where the human smiled and laughed through their days, the changeling only weeps and wails and complains.

MARGOT: I suppose now I can say it. I know you've never been happy with Stuart.

NAT: That's not true, Mum. I was happy with him, at first and then for a while after. I'm just not happy any more. Something changed. I don't know what.

MARGOT: You weren't happy, and I hated seeing you unhappy. It makes sense to leave.

NAT: Slow down! I just said I wasn't happy, I didn't say I was leaving him.

MARGOT: You didn't need to. I'm your mother, you don't think I know when you're happy? Those sad eyes, just like when you were little and I bought you the wrong colour birthday cake. You never said a word about it, just 'thank you', and then smiled as wide as anything. But I knew that it wasn't right.

NAT: It's not like that. I know I should be happy. I have everything and still it's not enough. It's as if he's given me all the treasures from all the oceans, but what I really want is a single dry stone.

MARGOT: So go out there and find your stone.

NAT: I can't build a life on a dry stone, Mum. No one would be happy with that.

MARGOT: Some people are happy with treasures and wide oceans. Some people are happy with a single stone. It doesn't matter what others want if it's not what you want.

NAT: No, I – Mum, I have to stay. I can't just leave him for no reason.

Changelings can be identified by several behaviours. These include: voracious appetite, malicious temperament, troubled movement, or unusual wisdom.

STU: I've figured it out. You have a brain tumour. In your prefrontal cortex. You need to go to hospital. Get eye tests and hearing tests. An MRI. A biopsy. X-rays. We'll find it, and we'll get rid of it. You'll be back to normal again.

NAT: You're trying to scare me.

STU: And are you scared? No. Because you've got a bloody brain tumour dictating all your emotions.

NAT: Stop being an arse.

STU: Symptoms of frontal lobe tumours include personality changes, mood swings, disinhibition, difficulty planning, and apathy. That's loss of interest in life.

NAT: Yes, because quoting an anatomy textbook at me is really going to help.

STU: Personality changes. Apathy. *Apathy*, Nat.

NAT: Enough.

STU: You don't care that your marriage is falling apart. If that's not apathy, what is? It explains everything.

NAT: Nothing explains everything.

STU: This does! Why else would you – would you suddenly change?

NAT: I haven't suddenly changed. And I'm not apathetic. Being unhappy isn't the same as apathy.

STU: Apathy means loss of interest in life. It means a loss of interest in our life together.

NAT: I know what it means.

STU: That's what you've got.

NAT: I have plenty of interest in life. Just not . . .

STU: . . . Just not with me?

NAT: You're getting upset.

STU: Because you're not!

NAT: It's just a trial separation. I want to see how it goes, if we can manage –

STU: This is the tumour talking.

NAT: I'm going out. I have to go and – I'm just going.

Changelings can be convinced to change places with the stolen human. The simple way to rid oneself of a changeling is to surprise it into revealing its true character.

NAT: Maybe I should go back. It makes sense to go back.

MARGOT: It makes sense to stay away from what makes you unhappy.

NAT: But how can I explain that to him when I don't understand it myself?

MARGOT: People aren't machines. They're not characters in books. You can't examine yesterday's actions and know for sure what they'll do tomorrow. People will always surprise you. There's no sense in trying to find the sense in it.

NAT: But I don't understand. There must be a reason. A marriage, a home – some people struggle their whole lives to get that. Why can't I be happy with it?

MARGOT: You know, Natasha, back when I left your father he couldn't take it. He said I was possessed. Bewitched. He tried to have me exorcised.

NAT: He did not.

MARGOT: Things were different then – divorce was unusual. I'd have none of it, of course. The priest came knocking at my door, and would I open it? I would not. I don't need a man flinging holy water over my clean dress and blowing perfumed smoke in my eyes, just because I didn't love my husband any more.

NAT: Was he crazy?

MARGOT: He was upset. He was confused. We all go a little crazy when our hearts are broken. He needed a reason.

NAT: What was the reason?

MARGOT: The reason was that loved him, and then one day I didn't. And there was no reason for that. I wasn't a machine, and neither are you.

Changelings can also be convinced by rougher methods, if softer approaches fail. These include being left bound out on the winter hillside, being placed on a hot stove, or being held under running water. When it comes down to it, beating and burning are the only reliable ways to deal with a changeling.

STU: I won't let you leave.

NAT: Don't be silly. Just get out of the way. I only came back to pack a few things. I'm not leaving you, it's just – I need something. I don't know what it is, but I can't find it here.

STU: No. You're not going.

NAT: Stu, for god's sake get your hands off me. Do you really think this is going to make me stay? When did a tantrum ever change anything? Did anyone ever change by force?

STU: No, I didn't mean to – I'm sorry, I won't touch you again. I shouldn't have – it's just that I figured it out, I know what this is. It's trauma. You're traumatised because of your father's death. My friend is a psychologist and he told me, he said he sees this sort of thing all the time at the practice.

NAT: Stop psychoanalysing me. It's not trauma. It's nothing to do with Dad, or my childhood, or my repressed anythings.

STU: Please. You must hear me. It makes sense. It's why you think you don't want your marriage any more.

NAT: I'm not traumatised.

STU: Then it's a tumour. Definitely. I know it. You're sick. You're not yourself. We have to get it fixed. I'll do anything to get you back to how you were. I'll drag you to the hospital if I have to.

NAT: Listen to yourself. Scrabbling around for reasons, like I'm a problem to be fixed. You sound insane.

STU: *I* sound insane? You're insane!

NAT: I know this might seem sudden to you, but –

STU: But nothing. We just got married. Literally just. And now you're walking out? You must have a tumour! It's the only explanation.

NAT: Fine, Stuart. Fine. If that makes you happy, that's what it is.

Changelings, some say, do not get the better side of the deal. They are never happy, but the stolen humans have plenty of good living and music and mirth in fairyland.

MARGOT: He was right? It is a tumour?

NAT: It's not a tumour. It's a – I don't know. A dark spot.

MARGOT: Do you want to go back?

NAT: No. I don't feel any different. But I have to, don't I? I can't leave him if he has a brain tumour.

MARGOT: You must do what's best for both of you. And if it's best to leave, you have to leave. If he changes back, will you love him again?

NAT: Did you ever love Dad again?

MARGOT: No.

NAT: But I have to go back now, Mum! I can't tell everyone my husband got a brain tumour – maybe a tumour, I don't know – and then I left him.

MARGOT: Oh, Natasha. You know that's not why.

NAT: No, but it – what will people say?

MARGOT: People will say what they say. Does it change how you feel? Can anything change how you feel? In the end, the reason doesn't matter.

Others say that despite the endless parties, the stolen humans lost in fairyland are not happy. They never give up on longing for their previous lives.

NAT: This is the last time. Here, have my key back, I won't need it again. You can call, okay, but I can't just pop in any time. Things are different now.

STU: They don't have to be.

NAT: Enough. I'm not talking about this again. I only came round to check you were okay.

STU: How kind of you. How ridiculously, sickeningly fucking sweet of you.

NAT: I don't need to know why you said that. Just don't say it again.

STU: Look, I'm sorry. I'm so sorry. For everything. I want . . .

NAT: What?

STU: I want to know why.

NAT: So do I. But I don't know. It's not that simple. Maybe I changed, maybe you changed.

STU: There has to be a reason. A better reason. Something I can fix.

NAT: It doesn't matter. You can say it's possession, you can say it's fairies or aliens, you can say it's trauma or a tumour. But the reason doesn't matter, because the result is the same. Whatever the reason, I'm still leaving.

Changelings may forget that they ever lived another life, and proceed to live this new life as if it were real. Even if they do remember, they may decide that their new life is preferable, and decide to keep it. In such cases, there is no chance of changing them back.

Liska / Ruth

– Liska, who are you talking to?

– No one. Just my own self. Go back to sleep.

– Were you talking to the baby?

– Yes. Caught me. I was saying good night, that's all. I know it's silly.

– You weren't. You were about to tell a story.

– I wasn't! We agreed that we wouldn't. Only truths.

– I've been thinking about that. Maybe we had the wrong idea. Maybe it's not a choice between truth and stories.

– I knew it! Ruth, my glorious wicked witch – you've been telling the baby stories, haven't you?

– No! Yes. But so have you.

– Not stories. Truths wrapped up in stories.

– I want to hear too. I wish I had heard all along. Tell me a truth, Liska. Please.

– Oh, if I must. Are you both listening? This is my last story. Long before I was born, my mama left Norway and travelled the world. I've told you about her first boyfriend, how he took her to that caravan roped up in the trees? She met him at her first job, one she ran away from the village to do. She ran away from that job for the boyfriend, and then she ran away again, from the boyfriend. Later she went back home to Norway, and met my dad, and she had me and my sisters, and she stopped running. She tried to pass it on to us, that stay-putting-ness, that everyday magic, like I'm trying to pass it on to the baby. My sisters didn't listen. They grew up into their own stories, dealt in their own ways. But my mama's lesson stuck with me. This is what she told me. This is the story I've lived by.

12
The Elephant Dance

I wouldn't exactly call it running away. The circus came and I was in the village; the circus left and I wasn't in the village. Who could resist the sawdust and the tightrope and the endless strings of glinting lights? Who could resist the strongman's waxed moustache and the acrobats' elastic limbs? Who could resist elephants? I didn't even bother with a suitcase.

I got all I expected: shimmer, sparkle, sleight of hand – and yes, elephants. But circus life isn't as glamorous as you'd think from storybooks and playbills. I got a lot of shit, and not just the sort the elephants dropped. Rounding up men rowdy on drink, shivering myself to sleep in the bible-black mornings. Once I misjudged my neat drop off the elephant's back and landed with the sickening gasp of a fractured bone. I had to keep my smile shiny-wide until I could get backstage; no one gets to see the cracks in the circus's painted face. Despite all that, there are good reasons to choose this life. No, that's not right: there is only one reason.

We've all done wrong.

Maybe it's impossible to escape from that, but constant movement made me feel as if I was getting further away from it. The circus is always shifting, gaining and losing someone in each new town: one person joins, needing to escape; another person leaves, tired of running. It might be enough for some to whitewash their mistakes, to hide them away like nothing ever happened. But not me. You'll never be shiny-new again, so why pretend? I wanted my mistakes glittered, tightrope-balanced, wrapped in gum-pink marabou. I wanted them lit up bright enough to dazzle heaven. No one up there could miss me, somersaulting and shimmy-shaking on the back of my elephant. Like I say, you can't go back to how you used to be. Might as well shrug on that sinner's mantle and rock it for all you're worth.

I've been gone for a while now, but I do remember home. After a while in the circus, it gets hard to see clear with glitter catching in every blink. But the further away I get, the better I can see it. Home: the star-prickled sky, the wooden houses painted bright as toys, the first snows smelling sharp as liquorice. Back then, I was too busy dreaming of circuses to see. I didn't understand that there's magic everywhere, if you look for it.

I didn't see the magic, so I couldn't help my sister to see. I didn't notice the beauty of our village, nestled snowily in its little cup of ocean. I stood with my back to it all, looking out at the road, waiting for the magic to come to me. But it didn't come. After a while it seemed that there was no magic left in the world – and what's the point of living in a world without magic? That's how the stink seeps in: when you forget to chase it out. It takes daily work, noticing magic. The mind likes to slip into mediocrity, and from there it's not far to misery. That's where my sister went. She chose her way out, and I wasn't watching, so it was too late for me to pull her back. All winter the rivers are lidded with ice; if you can smash your way into an entrance hole, you won't get an exit.

But that was a long time ago. Lifetimes ago. I got myself a new life, and it was glitz and fanfare and elephants. You have to be very careful on those broad dusty backs. You have to look. You have to see. Slip for just a moment, and the last thing you'll know is the underside of an elephant's foot.

Listen: When I said that we've all made mistakes, that sparked something in you, didn't it? A match-flare, a kicking up of dust. You know it's true, because you've done it too. You forgot to look. You didn't help others to see. Well, I'm here to tell you that there is a way out. No, that's not right: there are two ways. One was my sister's. The other is mine.

It's not too late. You can still learn. Fling your shoes into the lake, watch for the wolfishness in your neighbour's face, slip a pebble in your mouth to taste the sea, tilt your head up to see the stars. Look out for the magic.

Or the circus will come for you, and you'll never go home again.

Ruth/Liska

– Liska, that's what you want to tell the baby? That the world is full of magic?

– Yes. It's the most important thing I know.

– I'm glad. I want the baby to know that.

– Now it's your turn. Your last story. What do you want to tell?

– I can't, not with you here. It's too – do I have to?

– Yes, Ruth. You have to. Just close your eyes and talk, like you would if I wasn't here.

– But we agreed, about the stories. I feel like I've done wrong, lying to you.

– Are the stories lies?

– No. They're the truest things I know. I wouldn't lie to you, or to Coorie.

– Good! Now come in here, under my arm, and tell us a story.

– I'm ready. This is what I want to say. In the end, when it's all over, there are only two ways to die. Your heart or your lungs. One of them gives up. No matter what happens – drowning, car crash, heart attack, cancer. Your lungs stop inflating or your heart stops beating. And that's what you always felt like to me, Liska: my heart and my lungs. That's how vital you are to me. And now that's how Coorie feels like inside me. I'm keeping our baby alive, but our baby is keeping me alive too. I want to say that our baby will always have love, even after we're gone. Here is my last story, as true as I can make it.

13

The Ghost Club

There are things you need to know about the dead. The dead are not watching over us. The dead are not our friends. If a person did not yank you out of the path of a speeding truck or lead you to a cache of gold coins in life, they will not do so in death. Why would something as predictable as death change us? Dying does not transform a villain into a hero; not even an average man into an above-average man.

Our group meets in a church hall, but we're not religious. If we thought religion would help, we'd embrace it. But that is exactly the sort of thing we're trying to get away from at the meetings. The metaphysical. The unexplained, the inexplicable. Life after death. In anticipation of new members we wear handwritten badges: MY NAME IS. The chairs are hard plastic and the air smells of old lasagne. We drink weak coffee from a tartan Thermos. Sometimes there are doughnuts.

'Think of this as rationality recovery. A twelve-step programme to rid yourself of the drug of irrationality,' says Allison Fox, our fearless leader. Allison Fox is never anything more or less than Allison Fox: never Allison, never Ms. Fox, never Ally or Al.

Allison Fox is haunted by her dead child. It died three weeks before it was due to be born, and Allison Fox had to carry it around inside her for those three weeks before she could give birth, knowing it was dead. You wouldn't think it was possible for death to precede birth – they seem like opposite ends of a journey, beginning and end. But not for Allison Fox's baby.

'I'd like to share first, if I may.' That's Pawl. Pawl is haunted by his wife, who died suddenly of a brain tumour. One day she forgot the word 'teabag' and stumbled as she climbed the stairs, and six months later she went to sleep and never woke up. At night she writes in felt pen on the walls of his built-in cupboard. Pawl doesn't know for sure that the messages are from his wife as they're all in Cyrillic. The writing is always gone by morning. Pawl doesn't want to show it to anyone. He won't photograph it or copy it out. He is learning Russian so he can read the messages his wife leaves. His wife was Russian but she spoke perfect English, Pawl says. I think that if she wanted him to read the messages, she wouldn't write them in Russian. I don't say this to Pawl. We never question one another's ghosts. We know they're not real, and how can you wonder about what someone who wasn't there didn't do? Pawl gets unreadable messages in felt pen from his ghost, and Allison Fox feels the warm grasping babyfingers of her ghost, and I am awoken every midnight by the soft gaze of my ghosts. We know they're not real. But there they are. That's why we go to the meetings.

'You may begin, Pawl,' says Allison Fox.

Pawl tells us that he stayed up until three last night, waiting for his wife. He is quick to add that he was waiting not because he wanted her words, but so that he could disprove their existence. The words didn't come, and Pawl says he was glad.

Pawl is lying. We all lie. We bask in the comfort of our ghosts. We meet in this church hall to push our ghosts away, refusing to believe that this constant summoning of the dead only brings them closer.

Last week we had a new member. He was haunted by a medieval plague doctor. The doctor appeared at the foot of his bed in the darkest part of the night. He wore a leather mask and tarnished armour over a stained linen shirt. When the doctor leaned over the bed and exhaled, his breath smelled of the vinegar and rosewater-soaked sponges tucked in his cheeks. The man was so frightened he soiled himself. He's thinking of calling one of those ghost-hunting TV programmes, but he's afraid of soiling himself on camera. The man hasn't come to this week's meeting, and he won't be invited to next week's trip. We don't discuss those sorts of ghosts.

I'm sitting next to Pawl, so when he's finished with his half-truths he turns to me. I shake my head. Allison Fox looks at me for a few seconds, eyebrows raised. I raise mine back. She moves on.

Next is Caron. Caron is haunted by her grandfather too, which I sometimes find comforting. Caron's grandfather appears to her wherever temporary shapes can be found: in clouds, in stirred soup, in caffè crema, in waves licking up over the sand. Nothing that stays. Nothing that you can show. Usually it's his profile – that Roman nose, that strong brow – but sometimes it's his hands or his upper back. Caron is sure that it's him. We're all sure about our ghosts.

After that it's Jen and John and Gloria-Ann, haunted by their great-aunt and father and twin. We talk and we pretend to listen, and then we do a test. Last week it was a seance, but the man with the plague doctor kept shivering and wailing about how he could smell rosewater and vinegar. Allison Fox looked furious. Nothing is supposed to happen at the seances. No ghosts are supposed to appear, or to smell. That's the point. This week it's the Ouija board.

Allison Fox dims the lights while Caron and Pawl spark the candles, one for each of us. Fourteen fingers are too many for one glass so we use an upside-down pudding bowl. Allison Fox asks questions in a loud voice.

ARE THERE ANY SPIRITS IN THE ROOM?
CAN THE SPIRITS MAKE THEMSELVES KNOWN?
DO THE SPIRITS HAVE ANY MESSAGES FOR US?

The bowl does not move. We all stare at the muscles in one another's fingers to see if they flex. The muscles do not move. The bowl doesn't either.

Allison Fox flips the lights back on. We all blow out our candles, feeling vindicated. Ghosts aren't real, and we have proven it. Next week we will get on a bus and go on a trip to prove it again. For now, we say goodbye and go home to our ghosts.

I jolt awake. The clock glows 00:00. I feel eyes on me. My father, my grandfather. They're not looming over my bed. Not hovering by the ceiling. Just there. Just watching as I sleep cocooned between the walls and the floor and the ceiling they once slept between. I pull the covers over my head to hide. My own breath suffocates me. I push the covers away, kick them to the floor. Look, Dad; look, Grampa: my pyjamas are clean and my bed sheets are ironed and everything is fine so you can go. You can get out of my house. It's mine now because I inherited it, even though I didn't earn it. My father earned it, and my grandfather earned it before him. Every part of

this home was theirs. And now it's all mine, because they died. But
still they won't die.

There are more things you need to know about the dead. You need to
know more things than I can tell you. The dead keep their secrets and
they keep your secrets. They keep your secrets from other people, but
they can keep your secrets from you too. And they can do it forever
because the dead never, ever die.

This week we meet just outside the church hall, in the garden
of drooping roses, our shoes dusted with soil. When the minibus
arrives, we file on wordlessly. I sit beside Caron. I don't believe in
her grandfather's ghost but I still find it comforting, that connection.
We sit in companionable silence all the way to Glencoe. While the
countryside spools past the window, I pretend that tonight I will
return to an empty house. I imagine four walls enclosing me and
only me; silent, dreamless sleeps; space to breathe without the choke
of ghosts. I lean back against the headrest and wonder if Caron is
imagining this too, her own silent house.

The minibus parks up on a hill and we file off, clutching our
backpacks of equipment. EMF detectors, tape recorders, digital
thermometers. These are things used to record ghosts, which we will
use to show that you can't record what does not exist.

'Right, everyone,' announces Allison Fox. 'Let's split up. We'll
cover more ground that way.' It's like she's never seen a horror film.
It's the middle of the afternoon on a bright Sunday, but still.

Below us stretches a patch of ground, speckled with daisies and
dandelions. It's pretty. Quaint and rustic. This is where thirty-eight

people were violently killed at the Massacre of Glencoe. The Campbell clan murdering the MacDonald clan, in the days when clans meant more than which tartan to get on your keepsake bookmark from the gift shop.

'I think we should take opposite ends,' says Jen, with a big grin at John.

'Might be safer for us both, at least until you've officially joined the MacDonald clan,' says John, with a wink at Jen.

Jen Campbell and John MacDonald. They're engaged, and already this trip is becoming another episode in the grand epic of their romance. It hasn't even happened yet and already it's a cute story. The ancient battles show that those people were more into violence and death, while we modern sorts care more about peace and love. The dead were wrong and we are right. We will never be the dead.

I don't care where I go, as long as I don't have to be a side-character in Jen and John's romance. I stride off along the hilltop. The fuzz of Jen's EMF detector fades behind me. In its place there's birdsong, a shifting breeze, the shuffle of my feet on the grass.

I turn the volume of my EMF detector right down and switch on my tape recorder. The sun is warm on my neck. Below me flowers nod, fat clouds float above. Every five minutes I click off the tape, rewind it, and listen. I hear only birdsong, a shifting breeze, the shuffle of my feet on the grass. I turn the volume up as loud as it will go and hold the speaker to my ear, closing my eyes and pushing my hearing past those sounds, trying to hear something deeper. Something hidden. The screams of the dying, perhaps, or long-buried wails of grieving mothers. I hear nothing. There's nothing to hear. I smile and rewind the tape, ready for the next recording.

Every so often as I wander I bump into Pawl or Caron or Gloria-Ann. We nod politely to one another. Our calm smiles show that we have found exactly what we wanted to find, which is nothing at all. The afternoon passes in pleasant failure.

Later, we convene by the bus. The clouds have closed over us, dimming the light. We fidget with our non-haunted haunting equipment. We triumphantly play one another our tape recordings of silence and our own footsteps.

'I've got something!' gasps Jen. 'Voices, on my recorder.'

Allison Fox purses her lips. 'Are you sure, Jen?'

'Yes! Listen.'

We listen.

'Oh, that's just John,' says Gloria-Ann. 'You must have been standing near him.'

'But I wasn't!' says Jen. 'We split up, like we were meant to. He went all the way to the other side of the hill, where I couldn't even see him. If I couldn't see him, then how could this hear him?' She wields the tape recorder. She seems unsure whether to be proud or disappointed. 'And there's another voice, too. I think it's a woman. Listen.'

We look at John. He shrugs. We look at the tape recorder. The sound is crackly, but there are words under the fuzz, and it's unmistakably John's voice. His and another.

I miss you. I miss you.

We don't need to be impatient. This is real love. Just wait.

I know. Not long now. I love you too.

We look at John. He looks as if he's going to be sick. He slides his hand over his jeans pocket, over the denimed bulge of his mobile phone.

'Oh my God,' whispers Jen. 'Oh my God, John. A ghost was talking to you. Do you think she was a Campbell? Maybe it was a Campbell giving you advice for our wedding? Telling you ancient wisdom about love?'

Under Jen's awed babble, the recorded voices continue.

It's okay, I'm telling her soon.

I'll call when I can. Love you more than giraffes love leaves.

Jen is listening only to herself. On the tape, the voices stop talking. Hazy birdsong and the scuff of footsteps. We all look at John. He looks at the tape recorder.

'Well,' says Allison Fox. She clears her throat. 'Well. Let's head back. Next week we will be scrying with crystals. I think we did some good work today.'

00.00. Awake. Eyes. Dead fathers. I'm dreaming about sex with an ex. I wake with thighs tense, still grasping out for him. My cheeks feel hot. I try not to look guilty. My father is dead and my grandfather is dead, and even the dead can't know your dreams. Listen to me. Listen. You are dead and I want you to go. When my family were alive I never wanted them to die, but now they're dead I want them to die. Die, if that means they'll be gone. I don't need them now. I'm an adult. Can't they see that? An adult, hiding under the bed sheets.

There are things you need to know about the dead. But there are things to know about living too. There is a certain guilt in living, in being alive when other people are dead. The dead did not die because they were worse than you, or because they were better. They just died. Some time – maybe when you are very old but maybe when you are very young – you will just die too. And other people will live, and they will be guilty in turn.

At work I photocopy some papers and alphabetise some other papers and send emails about yet more papers. I plan how I can get rid of the ghosts that I do not believe exist. I imagine what it would be like to live in a house just big enough for me. A house with no space for ghosts, or for a lack of ghosts. I picture the empty walls and the silent midnights, the scent of nothing and the endless tick of hours. The lukewarm dinners. The single lit bulb.

I stop typing emails. My hands hover over the keyboard. I think about how I would be able to hear myself breathing. I think about how every sound I made – every sniff, every cough, every shuffle – would echo. I picture myself as a rowing boat, unmoored, drifting on the dark maw of the sea.

That night, when it's time for the meeting, I don't go. I'm tired of sneaky John and oblivious Jen. I'm tired of Caron and Pawl and Gloria-Ann and Allison Fox and all their ghosts, layer on layer of ghosts, grasping clammily at their hands, wailing for their attention. I'm tired of meeting in a draughty church hall and conjuring up ghosts, tracing over their outlines again and again, never letting them fade. I want to try something else.

I spend the evening at home. I wander the rooms, pressing my palms to the walls, bumping my knees on the cold radiators. After my grampa died, I felt like a different person. A sad girl in a story. It was a role to play, but when I got bored of playing my grampa didn't come back. Then my dad died, and I realised that no floor was steady, no wall was sturdy. The world was stage dressing, flimsy as plywood.

From them I inherited a floor and some walls, and I hoped that they would feel solid when nothing else did. As I wander I think about everyone I know who is haunted. If Allison Fox's baby hadn't died, maybe she would be Ally. If Pawl's wife was alive, maybe he wouldn't be learning Russian, and there would always be a language separating them. Our ghosts make us who we are. When we do not like our ghosts, we do not like ourselves. If no one ever died, maybe we would never learn what it meant to miss them. Maybe then we would not learn how to live a life that would be missed. By the time I've made it around the edge of every room, the walls seem to lean a bit less.

I watch a TV quiz show, calling out the answers to show my dad that I know, that my education gave me an excellent general knowledge. I look through old photos of my granddad as a boy, knee-high on a rugged hillside, tousle-haired and gap-toothed in black-and-white, playing with his two brothers, the three of them piled on a single bicycle, going camping in shorts and peaked caps. I sing along to the radio as I make dinner: lean protein, plenty of vegetables, spices; to show them that I understand my need for both nutrition and taste. I put on my clean pyjamas and slip into my clean bed.

These walls. This floor. My father and grandfather are in them, making them strong, making them steady. Perhaps the rest of the world is only stage dressing, but these walls will grow solid if I let them. I fall asleep, ready to meet my ghosts at midnight.

I wake the next morning to the sun warming my face. I haven't closed the curtains since moving in – there was no point, as I'd be woken long before dawn would disturb me. But not now. Now I stretch out, luxuriating in the cool space beyond the reach of my feet. I could sleep more, but I won't. I'll get up and put on a pot of coffee and boil eggs for breakfast. Tonight, I will sleep again.

There is really only one thing you need to know about the dead, and it's that they are dead. They can't come back to comfort us. But still they comfort us.

Acknowledgements

A note on 'Cold Enough to Start Fires': This story is inspired by a journal that my father, Ewan Logan, kept on a family holiday taken when I was five. Although none of the characters in the story are based on people from mine or Ewan's lives, several images and phrases in the story are taken directly from the journal. I am grateful to him for many things, including this co-writing.

Thank you:

Duncan Jones at ASLS; the family of Gavin Wallace, particularly Pauline, Patrick, Ali and Morag; Cathryn Summerhayes and Siobhan O'Neill at WME; Liz Foley, Alison Hennessey, Bethan Jones, Vicki Watson, Áine Mulkeen and Helen Flood at Penguin Random House; Aly Barr at Creative Scotland; Caitrin Armstrong and Claire Marchant-Collier at Scottish Book Trust; Susie McConnell, Helen Sedgwick, Katy McNair and Paul McQuade for feedback; Alasdair and Alison Macleod for the fishing boat; Mama Bennett and Uncle Peter for the holiday park and the animal birthday party; and Annie Bennett-Logan, Mama Logan and Ross Logan for absolutely everything.

A Portable Shelter was made possible with the support of Creative Scotland's Dr Gavin Wallace Fellowship. Gavin was an inspiration and a support to me and many other writers, and I am proud to have his legacy attached to this book.

penguin.co.uk/vintage